LEGACY

LEGACY

A First Novel

DAVID A. NOVELLI

ISBN-13: 9781517715984
ISBN-10: 1517715989
Library of Congress Control Number: 2015916652
CreateSpace Independent Publishing Platform
North Charleston, South Carolina

PREFACE

My father died in 1989 as the personal computer was becoming common. Tasked with helping my mom with his records, I discovered his several attempts at writing on an early desktop computer. The words in amber predated the sophisticated graphical user interfaces that we've come to enjoy. I've saved these files and can still access them today, twenty-five years later, on my own desktop. He'd attempted to write some poems and a book entitled, *The Family*. He'd completed a draft of four chapters of his book. As I read the pages then, I heard my deceased father's voice: something I wish I could actually hear again. The words he had composed were and remain priceless. Finding them inspired me to someday give my own attempt at writing. Perhaps when I am gone, my own children will be able to hear my voice as they read this story about legacy.

Legacy is a business-fiction novel, but it is not about business. I hope you figure out what it is about, and if and when you do, I hope it informs the way you approach the business of your own life. Here's a hint: we have an impact whether we know it or not. The secret is in figuring out how to see the impact and learning how we can transmit this impact into action.

ACKNOWLEDGMENTS

I wish to offer heartfelt thanks to my close and dear friends who have taken time from their own very busy lives and schedules to help me with this project.

Many thanks to Marissa Kennerson, who provided a professional touch to my first draft. I learned immensely from her, watching her first take the story apart and then create a "treatment." I had never heard the word used this way, but I learned that this is an approach to organizing the events of a story in a way that guides the writer's production. I was also amazed at how you can take narrative and turn it into a dialogue, which made the story much more interesting than "boy walks dog; dog chases car; boy falls down." You can change that to: "'Bo, let's go for a walk. Go along now, grab your leash!' the boy said to his best friend as the dog's tail wagged in a circle. The circle wag was always the best of all wags that Bo offered his beloved master." Then you make a story more like a novel, to the enjoyment of all. Marissa also earned her pay by putting a woman's touch on things. She gave life to characters I had brushed over and even produced a few more. Without Marissa, love and its alter ego, grief, would never have emerged the way they have. And finally, I think she balanced things out. I think a woman might like this novel now, thanks to Marissa.

I also want to thank key contributors. Nancy McGuire, my sister, read one of the early efforts at our ranch while sitting by a pool. She labored through several chapters before the story grabbed her attention, and then she rallied through the rest of it. Steve Blake, one of my pallbearers, told me there was no tension and that every story is elevated by tension, giving rise to some of the dark corners of our characters' journeys. Kevin Kuykendall, who after reading the beginning was eager to have more, enthusiastically encouraged me because he desperately wanted to know what happened next. He also, incidentally, actually knows Spanish. Matt Kuryla is a great biblical and Roman Catholic scholar who masquerades as an environmental lawyer. He provided excellent comments and a thinking man's reflection. Don King is always insightful, thoughtful, and encouraging, and he never fails to see the best in others! Don helped me make the ending better. To all of these pals, I say **THANK YOU**! You guys are much cheaper than professional writers, editors, and the like, and your feedback is in many ways more meaningful because it is offered where it belongs—right between the eyes.

PROLOGUE

I am resting. My head is back against the seat, and my thoughts flow freely, drifting to the hum of the engines as the aircraft flies with the jet stream. The lights are dimmed, and many of the passengers are sleeping. But even while my body is at rest, my mind is racing.

A hand rests gently on my shoulder. "Sir, we'll be landing shortly. Is there anything else I can get you?"

Used to such interruptions, I slowly open my eyes as if coming to, even though I am very much awake. I look up at her, pausing and admiring. She is a young Hispanic woman whose beauty glows through her olive skin and radiant, dark eyes. Her hair is pulled tight in a ponytail, and she is wearing fashionable glasses. She's in a navy-blue suit with a Salvatore Ferragamo scarf and a pin of our flag. She's wearing a dark shade of lipstick—red, but not too bright. There is a beauty mark above her right cheek that reminds me of the American actress Elizabeth Taylor. As I admire her, she reminds me of someone else in the memories I've been stirring. Slowly, I force a smile.

"No. Thank you," I say.

"Sir?"

"Yes?"

"Are you OK?"

I pause, looking at her. My eyes meet hers, and her face slowly melts away a pain that has been lurking. There is grief in my eyes, I am sure, and she seems genuinely concerned.

"Yes, I'm fine."

"We'll be landing in about forty minutes. Do you want to review anything? Should I call any of the others over?"

I quickly raise my hand as I realize that what she senses is miles away from what I am feeling. "No, no…I have no concerns about that…I was just reliving something that happened a long time ago. I am ready…and excited! Today is a very good day." Now my smile is genuine, and I hope my energy is inviting. I really am excited!

"Sir, I just want to say…I mean, well, thank you for all of this…"

"No, the thanks are mine. This is a team effort. None of us would be here without the others. Thank *you*!" I want to draw people in, compliment them, and build them up. She blushes. I bet that in her heart, she feels something much deeper. I think we are all thinking what a great gift it is to be part of this. We both smile at each other, and then as people do when they have no more words to offer, she nods gently, smiles, and lets out a breath. She steps away. She seems joyful.

I close my eyes and travel back to my memories. I start from the beginning. The years have faded away much of the detail. There was a time when I remembered every moment, every second. But in a way of healing and easing grief, only certain elements come to mind in great detail, and some of these details still haunt me even after all of these years.

I remember how much fun we were having and always had. I remember how much love I felt and what an influence this love had on me, then and today. I was ten years, nine months, seven days old. I know because everyone always knows the exact time and place something so impactful happens. We were smiling and laughing but not talking. It had been a good night. As we exited the building where my mother worked that evening, things seemed very peaceful. I remember it being cool. It wasn't uncomfortable, but there was a chill in the air. These were some of the foggier memories.

What I remember in vivid detail was the smile on the man's face as he approached us. I remember smiling back, too. My God, I smiled back! That memory is the one that hurts the most. The smile is so perfectly vivid now, because in hindsight some thirty years later, I know the smile was a devious one. In fact, I've learned to read smiles as if they are the fine print. My success has come, in part, from this ability to look into a man's heart and by the way he smiles, choose friends and identify enemies. This is an important skill in my line of work. You don't get here without knowing which people are which and being careful in how you engage with each, friends and enemies.

I remember at that moment being pushed hard and falling to the ground. As I fell back, the palms of my hands stung. That's where my mind was in the confusion—my hurting palms. This makes me sick, and it also makes me laugh at the sadness of the moment. I was so innocent, simple, and unaware that I smiled at a man who, while smiling back, threw me to the ground. And in that moment, I was worried about my palms. God, forgive me for that!

I was probably looking down at them; I'm not sure, and I don't remember exactly what happened next. There was a tussle between the man and my mother, and the scuffle caused me to look up. As I did, I sensed the evil threat.

My mother was wrestling to keep her bag, and the man was trying to take it, pulling it from her. I jumped up and ran hard into the man. But hard is a relative thing. Mass and speed determine the force of impact, and as hard as I ran into the man, trying to push him away, my 70 pounds had little effect on his 225 pounds.

He didn't budge. Instead, he just became agitated and used all of his force to thrust me away. I remember my whole body hurting as I slammed to the ground. I've prayed so often about this because it was a terrible mistake summoned out of fear and shock and instinct, but had I stayed on the ground, perhaps things would have ended differently. It was only when I was pushed violently the second time that my mother became hysterical.

She must have wanted to protect me and in doing so was fighting with what little strength she had. He had moved past agitated to ballistic at all of this and grabbed her, perhaps by the shoulders and the waist, and literally held her torso in the air as her arms flailed back and forth. And then, as clear as day, I remember seeing her flying through the air with her back to the ground, and her hands following behind her as if in slow motion, but in what was probably only a second or two. I remember it in vivid detail. I still can see her beautiful hair blowing as she sailed. Her mouth gaped as she breathed in, and I can see her head as it hit the wall across the alley. I remember the thud of her hitting the wall and the stunned silence that came next—all as I lay on the ground.

The man looked at her like she was a sack of potatoes that had fallen and broken open. "Good riddance" is what his face said. Good riddance. As God is my witness, I will never forgive the man for such disdain.

The man leaned down to look through the purse where it had fallen to the ground. I was frozen with fear. I never heard what happened next, but I remember it. In less than a minute, the tide turned as I sat there in shock. An angelic figure, it seemed, had come to our rescue. By God's grace another man appeared there, and despite the pain of these memories, I am here.

BOOK ONE
WRONG PLACE, WRONG TIME

ONE

The air was heavy and wet—some would say thick and unpleasant—but it was typical for a late summer day on the coastal plains that line the Texas Gulf Coast. Cloud cover provided some relief from the sun, but it left the day gray and lackluster.

"Oh shit!" Jim Swanson was exhausted. His fair skin was reddened with exertion, and his locks of thick, sandy-brown hair, grayed at the temples, were slicked back with sweat. There was a small breeze, but it was no match for the heat and did little to offer any reprieve. Up ahead, Jim spotted a hill.

"This is crazy. Why is there a hill here?" he thought grimly. He was hot, tired, and almost entirely depleted. "I can't do it." He was sore, his feet were burning, and his body was aching.

Jim looked around him. Now into the third hour, it was clear the event was wearing on Jim's competitors as well. The group had started the day in the dark by boarding a large ferry at six o'clock in the morning. From there, the vessel had carried them to the middle of Galveston Bay, near the pathway to the Houston Ship Channel, which carried the country's third largest vessels. Daily ships carried petrochemicals, grains, and other commodities through this channel of water.

A mile across the water was the shoreline. It wasn't much to look at. What were once native banks, weedy and overgrown, were now overdeveloped. Jim and the others swam straight to shore, transitioned to their bicycles, and rode on the highways and local roads before coming back to the small town of Kemah.

Kemah could be described as a smaller and more manicured Coney Island. Its boardwalk boasted rides and was dotted with restaurants and shops. From the ferry, swimmers could see a huge Ferris wheel, a rotating tower, and the roller coaster. While the town was a tourist attraction, it also had a very close-knit community that had made a special effort to come out and welcome the race participants.

The last leg of the race was a six-mile run, and the Heartbreak Hill Jim had seen welcomed the runners at mile five. It was a true ballbuster that had to be conquered in order to finish the race.

Jim was tired, but a faint rhythm drummed beneath his movements, providing some kind of autopilot momentum. He'd been here before. He was not new to challenges; his life had carried its share of obstacles—be they physical, emotional, or otherwise—but he was getting older, and on this particular morning, he was feeling it. Life had begun to take its toll while he wasn't paying attention.

There were a lot of men and women out here who were in better shape, fit and able to knock out an Olympic-distance triathlon like a Sunday workout. Jim was not one of them. But, to be fair, for a fifty-three-year-old guy with a job like his, he was pretty damn fit.

"Fifty-four years old," he reminded himself. Today was his birthday, and his wife, Anita, was home preparing for a blowout at their house this evening. Everyone was sure to ask about the race, and he had better have a good story to tell. No quitting now. Jim took a deep breath and gathered himself.

Triathlons were a great reason to stay in shape. They forced him to stay on track. Jim wasn't the only one. In the 1970s, running had become popular in the United States. But in more recent years, triathlons were gaining in popularity. Competitors began with a swim, usually in open water, followed by a bicycle race over local roads, and ended with a run. There were generally four classes of races: The shortest races were sprints, which took about an hour to complete; they included a 300- to 500-meter swim, a 12- to 18-mile bike ride, and usually a 5-kilometer run. The more demanding events were Olympic-distance races involving a 1600-meter swim, a 40-kilometer bike ride, and a 10-kilometer run. But the real pros were the ironmen, who could complete a 2.5-mile swim in open water followed by a 120-mile bike ride and a 26.2-mile marathon. Some people took ten or twelve hours to complete these grueling ultraendurance events. The world champions could knock them out in fewer than eight hours.

For Jim, like many of the other competitors over thirty, the sprint- and Olympic-distance competitions had become the race of choice. He found himself in good company with postcollegiate athletes, high-energy type A people—the freaks who managed a workout before five o'clock in the morning—and a host of other regular folks just trying to heed their doctor's advice and find ways to exercise.

Of course, weaving through every race were women who came to look good in bathing suits and men who appreciated their efforts. It provided a singles scene for the middle-aged set that mercifully took place outside of the bars. People watching the connections particularly enjoyed the markings on the left calves, where race organizers marked the age of a competitor in big, blue numbers. It was done to help competitors know whether someone in their same age group was ahead of them. Age groups established how all rankings and winners were selected.

As Jim neared the hill, he realized it was the bridge under which large sailboats entered Galveston Bay. He began to find his fortitude. He just had to find a way to use the hill, or bridge, to his advantage. Others ahead were still running it, but they might as well have been walking. He noticed a high school kid climbing the bridge with his head down, defeated but moving forward. The boy's running seemed so laborious it was more of a shuffle. Jim knew this wasn't the answer.

"Think. If I walk the bridge, I might be able to stretch my stride, extend my stride up the slope, and give my legs some rest," he told himself. As he did this, he searched his body for feedback. The bridge was rising, but his strides became longer. Brilliant! It was working. He had reached a long, full walking stride and was moving rather quickly. He became more refreshed and grew stronger by the minute.

As he continued up the hill, he began passing runners. He wasn't moving *that* fast, but because of the strain of the bridge and the long race, the others were running *that* slow. He allowed himself to imagine the feast Anita was having brought to the house this evening: steaming trays of everything he loved best and then some.

"Not bad for an old man." Jim hummed to himself under his breath. He had this. His light blue eyes sparkled with quiet glee. He was in the flow. The race wasn't over, and it was hot—really hot. But he knew the worst of it was behind him. He noticed how good he felt. In a recent appointment, his doctor had told him to pay attention to his moods and what triggered them. From what he could tell, if he was being physically engaged, the strange sort of dullness he'd been experiencing lately couldn't touch him. Like now.

Last week, he had gone to his internist for his yearly physical. While he was there, he had confessed to his longtime doctor that he'd been experiencing a sort of lethargy. Something sort of gray had been playing around the edges of his day. It was unlike anything he had ever experienced before.

After running tests and finding out he was in tip-top shape physically, Jim laughed when his doctor suggested over the phone a few days later that Jim might be experiencing some low-grade depression.

"I'm an investment banker, Gary. We don't do depression."

"That may be true, Jim. But something is going on with you. Listen, I'm going to prescribe a light antidepressant. Watch your moods closely in the next few weeks. See what makes you feel good and what drags you down. Keep the pills, and if you can't shake this, just take them for six months. You'll see a world of difference."

Antidepressants. *That* was not going to happen. Jim had never heard of something so absurd.

As Jim crested the top of the hill at last, his legs gained a second wind. With less than a mile to go, he started running again, but this time with renewed energy. At six foot two and 210 pounds, he was a big man. He felt people turn to look at him as he began to pass them.

Jim breezed past the high school kid, who was still trying to run it out. He began to pick off other competitors, too. No one would pass Jim after this. He was locked on finishing strong. No sprint or kick—those days were over—but he wouldn't collapse like he had in the New York City Marathon, either.

That had been embarrassing. He was twenty-seven then and had run sub three hours. Today, Jim was still mentally tough and fiercely competitive, but now, almost thirty years later, he was more cautious and knew how to manage to his limits.

After the race, Jim made his way through some of the post-race concession booths. Volunteers offered waters, sports drinks, juices, bananas, pizzas, and power bars. He ran into a few friends and chatted about the race, asking them about their times or how they felt during the event.

Jim bumped into an old colleague named Charlie, whom he'd not seen in years. "Jim, do you know when we can get our bikes?"

"I think they'll keep the transition area closed until the last of the cyclists have returned and all of the competitors are either finished or on the run portion of the race." Jim looked at his watch. "I'd say in the next half hour."

"What do you have going on this afternoon?" Jim asked his friend.

"My daughter has dance class, and I am hoping to make it."

"That's great! How old is she?"

"She's eleven. She takes ballet, and I like to go with her. It helps her mom, too, to get a break for the afternoon. If they let us grab our gear in the next half hour, I'll make it no problem."

"Do you have any other children, Charlie?"

"We stopped at one, with Marsha working and all, but she's a handful!" Charlie said, smiling.

"Enjoy those dance classes. Time goes by fast, and you'll relish these days; trust me, I know. Mine are all grown up, if you know what I mean! Listen, Charlie, it was good to see you. I hope we can both keep doing these. I am going to grab something to eat and then get on the road myself. Be well!" Jim said as they shook hands.

Jim eventually grabbed his gear and made his way to the car. He was feeling replenished and good about his day. It was a ways to the parking lot where he'd parked his car. He was carrying a backpack on his shoulder and walking through the lot when he saw a woman trying to load her own bike into her hatchback. She seemed to be having a bit of trouble.

"Can I give you a hand?" asked Jim.

"My boyfriend put the bike in last night...I can't fit it. I think I'm doing something wrong," the woman said.

"Let me take a look." Jim assessed the car's back, looked at the bike, and thought that if the front tire came off, it would fit easily. "How did you do today?"

She smiled from ear to ear. "I finished! This is my first triathlon, and I've never done anything like it. I can't believe I was able to complete it."

"That's fantastic! I bet you keep doing them, too. The first one is the hardest, and I found after that I was hooked. It's such a great way to stay in shape, even for old guys like me! I have a suggestion on your bike. If we flip these levers here, we can release your front tire. It's pretty simple to put back together by just sliding it on when you get home. Have you done this before? I can show you how to do it."

After a try or two, the woman had the reassembly down. They took the tire off and laid the bike carefully in the back of her car. Jim helped her load the rest of her stuff, bid her farewell and good luck in the future, and made his way to his own car. It had been a successful morning and Jim was feeling great!

TWO

1:56:31-truly fantastic!

As Jim steered his brand-new Mercedes CLS Coupe, with his
$6,000 tri bike on the back, onto Interstate 45 toward Houston,
he congratulated himself. The car, which was painted a sleek,
deep, metallic, lunar blue, had been an early birthday present
from Anita. It drove like a dream and responded with both vim
and vigor when his foot punched the accelerator toward home.

Home.

Anita.

He couldn't wait to tell her about the race. They had both been
so busy lately—ships in the night. The more he thought about her,
the more he suddenly couldn't wait to see her.

Jim ran his fingers over the glossy walnut wood of the dash-
board, trying to find the radio without taking his eyes off the road.
The salesman, spurred on by Anita, had looked at Jim with excitement flashing in his eyes. He'd said things like, "Voice-activated
navigation and weather reports; intelligent, adaptive cruise control..." But Jim hadn't been paying attention. He had been busy
with his Blackberry, and to tell the truth, these sorts of details
annoyed him. He would enjoy the car, but Anita was the one who
made these sorts of decisions in their lives, and he was thankful for

that. It left his mind free to concentrate on more important things. He had once read that President Obama only had four varieties of suits, and an assistant picked out his daily wardrobe so that Mr. Obama himself didn't get decision fatigue. Jim might not share his politics, but the man knew a thing or two about success.

Jim finally managed to get the damn thing on. "Dream a Little Dream of Me," sung by Ella Fitzgerald and Louis Armstrong, took him by surprise as he felt himself instantly transported back to 1970 and the one-story, ranch-style home where he had grown up in Sharpstown, a modest blue-collar suburb of Houston. He remembered that very song playing as clearly as if it were yesterday. He was fourteen years old, and his mother was teaching him to dance.

While Jim stumbled around the kitchen, trying not to step on his mother's dainty feet, his father, Joseph Swanson, sat at the kitchen table surrounded by textbooks. Joseph worked as an automobile mechanic during the day and attended school at night, working to finish his bachelor's degree. Joseph was a good father, but he was always hard at work and preoccupied.

But that morning had been different. As Ella and Louis crooned through the radio that Jim's mother had set on the kitchen counter, Joseph had slammed his books shut with a smile.

"Let me show you how it's done, son." Jim's mother, Susan, smiled her beautiful smile, exposing her pretty white teeth. Her pale-blue eyes lit up as Joseph took her in his arms and began to lead her around their matchbox kitchen. As Jim watched, he could tell they were somewhere else altogether.

Jim shook his head at the memory. His dad had always worked so hard. He had busted his tail his whole adult life to make a better life for his family. He managed to put Jim and his younger brother, Luke, through parochial schools and then a Jesuit high school.

But at what expense? Jim's mother had been lonely, and the kids had never seen their father. And the worst part was that Joseph Swanson never really got ahead. Jim began to feel a dull feeling in his chest. The euphoria of the race began to fade away.

"Damn it," he said out loud. Thinking about his father always left him feeling an unpleasant mix of guilt and remorse. Jim was so deep in thought he nearly missed the exit toward home.

Thinking about his parents and their marriage made Jim think about his own marriage to Anita. He laughed out loud to himself as he changed lanes to pass a minivan plodding along in the fast lane. Thinking of his mother, Susan, and Anita in the same mental space made him chuckle. He certainly hadn't married his mother. Susan, may she rest in peace, had been quiet, sweet, and maternal, from a blue-collar family. The oldest of six, to hear her tell it, she had been a mother since the day she was born. Not so with Anita.

Anita Torino.

Anita was a legend in the elite Houston social scene, firmly establishing this status in high school. She was rich. Rich with a capital *R*. Anita's family owned several banks across Southeast Texas, including in towns like Victoria, Brownsville, and Laredo, catering to old Texas ranching families, oil and gas operators, and blue-collar entrepreneurs who'd built small businesses into small fortunes with the help of the Torino family. If Jim's dad hadn't busted his butt to pay for Jim's attendance to the prestigious Jesuit academy, Anita and Jim would never have encountered each other. They were from two different worlds.

They had their socioeconomic divide, but there was another divide between them as wide as it was deep. On the high school social strata, Anita was at the top: homecoming queen, head cheerleader—things that don't matter as much to kids these days, but in Jim and Anita's day, they had meant everything. She had driven a brand new car, and her clothing practically had its price tags intact. Jim, on the other hand, had been lucky to attend a private school, given the tuition costs. And for all her social star power, Jim was far from popular. He was just another student blended into the crowd.

Jim remembered the first time he saw her. It had been pouring rain, and the entire school had moved into the gymnasium for the pep rally. He had been caught completely off guard; he was ready to be bored out of his mind. Pep rallies weren't his idea of a good time. He was a wisp of a thing back then, and sports would come later for him. Don McLean's "American Pie" began to play over the gymnasium speakers. The pom-pom girls, easily the prettiest girls in the sister school, began to sashay toward the center of the gym, their short skirts twirling, their white gloves moving rhythmically to the music.

And then there she was. The girls converged around her. Raven-black hair pulled back into a thick high ponytail, olive skin, and impossibly large brown eyes. It was as if every other girl in Texas had been born blond-haired and blue-eyed to stand in contrast to, and highlight, Anita. They spun; they moved their hips provocatively. The music, the girls—they whipped the crowd into a frenzy of good feeling.

When the music slowed, Anita had sauntered toward the audience and taken the hand of Mike Brown, star quarterback, and, as everyone knew, her boyfriend. The other girls formed a circle around the couple, who swayed slowly to the music until it ended. Mike dipped Anita gallantly, and the place went crazy with applause. The girls threw their legs up with kicks, and everyone shouted, "*Vikings!*"

Jim hadn't stood a chance with her. She was out of his league in every way.

Anita was born with a silver spoon in her mouth, and she could have whatever she wanted. She had the world by the tail, and what Anita had wanted was to become Mrs. Mike Brown. They were *the* couple. Their families were practically identical. Their future was written.

But something had happened the summer between their senior year and college, and Jim had gotten a break. The door to Anita opened a crack, and he had been there to wedge his foot in. Jim had befriended Anita in quiet ways over the years. They both participated in the Jesuit Players Group, which drew actors from both the Jesuit academy and its sister school. Jim was good at getting Anita to sit still long enough memorize her lines. He was there to listen when she and Mike had a fight. Jim's friends thought he was pathetic, but he didn't care. Any possible way to be around Anita was preferable.

Mike left for a trip to Europe after high school graduation. The plan was for Mike and Anita to attend Southern Methodist University in the fall, where they would rule the Greek scene the way they had ruled high school. After college they would marry straightaway. But Mike fell in love with a Parisian girl that summer, which rocked his world and changed the course of things for all of them.

The exit for Shepherd Road popped up, pulling Jim's attention back to the present. He pulled off the highway with a feeling of excitement bordering on anxiety. Thinking about those early times with Anita made him realize how much they had grown apart lately, but also how much he loved her. He felt slightly aroused thinking of Anita and her strong brown legs against the lily white of her pom-pom uniform.

He'd pulled into the driveway a thousand times, and each time, he reflected on the beauty of their home. It was only a few miles from where he'd grown up in Sharpstown, but the two areas provided stark contrast. This had never been a modest area. His house was set among other mansions on the revered South Boulevard, a street lined with massive, old oak trees that reached above the road to enclose it in a canopy below which expensive cars traveled. The house had been built in the 1940s for one of Houston's elite oil men. It was English Tudor revival style, with a long, stretched elevation appointed by numerous gables, topped with a slate roof. To move through the driveway to the back, one passed under a porte cochere. Behind the main house was a second carriage house, which easily held four cars and an entire apartment above. In the days of Houston's first oil boom, near the time Spindle Top in nearby Beaumont blew its first oil gusher, this home would have been built from the black gold oil became. The yard was large enough that some might say the house had grounds, with perfectly manicured hedges shaded by numerous old oak trees, common in this part of Houston.

"Mike Brown," Jim said aloud as he pressed the opener for their gate. As the gate's heavy black wrought-iron doors—hand-picked by Anita—parted, Jim took a glance at himself in the rear-view mirror. He thought about this morning's race time, put his hand through his thick hair, and felt quite certain that today Mike Brown was fat and balding and probably a total loser.

THREE

When Jim entered the kitchen, Anita was clad in black yoga pants and a clingy pink tank top, obviously fresh from a workout. She wasn't skinny; she never had been. She was voluptuous and had maintained her shape well. In her early fifties, she had certainly aged, but she was still beautiful and would always be glamorous. She was struggling with the juicer and didn't notice Jim come in. He walked behind her and put his arms around her invitingly. She jumped.

"Gross! Jim! You're all sweaty." She struggled out of his embrace. Jim laughed.

"So are you, sexy." She frowned at him in response and gestured toward the juicer.

"You would think a six-hundred-dollar juicer would work!" Anita said, exasperated. As Jim adjusted the blender on the Vitamix, he felt himself deflate a little. He poured green juice for both of them, and as he was about to tell her about his race time, she kissed him perfunctorily on the cheek and dashed out of the room, calling instructions for the party over her shoulder.

"I have a million things to do. Be dressed and ready by six! Oh! And happy birthday, Jim!" she said.

"Thanks," Jim said to an empty room as he finished his juice. He opened the fridge. "Now for some real food." He realized he was famished.

◆ ◆ ◆

Showered and dressed for his party, Jim watched from his bedroom window on the second floor as the valet company Anita had hired for the night set up. Young guys were having fun and obviously ribbing one another, unaware that anyone was watching. One even took out a football, and they began to toss it around the expanse of the Swansons' front lawn. Jim raised his eyebrows in surprise but felt a small pang of jealousy. He was contemplating going down and joining them, even if for just a few minutes, when Anita appeared by his side, offering him a chilled vodka martini. She was stunning in a strapless cream cocktail dress made of crepe with a black lace peplum effect at the waist that highlighted the silhouette of her hourglass figure. Her hair was pulled back in a low bun, and large, diamond-stud earrings sparkled from her ears. Around her neck was a single diamond pendant. She looked luminous. Gone was the harried Anita from earlier today. She put her arm through his and smiled up at him, revealing perfect white teeth.

"Happy birthday, Darling. Looks like we're on." Anita nodded toward the drive where guests were being escorted up the long walkway that led to their front door. Jim nodded in response, taking a long sip of his cocktail. "Darling, don't be pissed about this afternoon." Anita pressed her full lips out in a mock pout. "I'll make it up to you later. For now, let's go greet our guests. They are here to celebrate with you!"

"Of course." Jim smiled, but he felt that damn dullness in his chest. What he really wanted to do was change into sweats and pop on the television. "What was that all about?" He just wasn't in a party mood. "Too late for that now," he thought. He followed Anita down the curve of the staircase that led to the foyer, where hired men and women in black tuxedos were taking people's coats and offering them flutes of champagne as a welcome.

Guests stepped onto the antique Italian marble floor and into the foyer. The tiles had been imported a few years earlier by Anita, who'd discovered them in a shop just outside of Paris. They were salvaged from a townhouse near the Champs-Élysées that was being torn down for a new hotel. The floor, like the sideboard across from the rolling staircase, was an extension of Anita's work, and her intent was for her clients to see the caliber of her own decorating vision as well as that of the sources she could access on their behalf. The sideboard was a seventeenth-century mahogany double-serpentine piece, with a well-worn gold inlay trim and a perfectly preserved burled-wood finish. On the sideboard sat a Louis XIV ormolu-mounted white-marble striking mantle clock. Draping down the center of the foyer was a huge crystal chandelier bought at a Sotheby's auction that had once been owned by a cousin of Henry Clay Frick, the benefactor of the famous Frick Collection. Not quite as famous or as rich as Henry, his cousin's family had done well in their time, too, and the lighting piece came from one of their Manhattan townhouses. Besides the guests and the servers, nothing else decorated the room. It was elegant and expensive, but edited, not cluttered. Anita's approach was to ensure everything in the homes she decorated was authentic— nothing but the best. She never sought a cluttered or busy look.

"There he is!" said a barrel-chested man who was approaching Jim and Anita. Pete Matli was well heeled, but his hair always seemed to be an unnatural shade of yellow. Anita beamed at her longtime tennis acquaintance from her childhood country club. Anita adored Pete, and Jim put up with him, as is often the case for spouses. To Jim, Pete was basically harmless, but he had always worried about Pete's character, which he sensed was less than impeccable.

"Peter," Jim said. Jim stood a good three inches above Pete. Anita and Pete immediately erupted into chatter about club gossip. Jim took the opportunity to really look at Pete. He stood a little too close to Anita for Jim's liking and touched her in a way that Jim found overly familiar.

Pete must have felt Jim watching and brought the conversation back to Jim. "Fifty-four. How does it feel to be getting old, Big Fella?" Pete laughed a thick, coarse laugh, and Anita conspired by poking Jim's stomach, which despite his fitness level had some softness to it.

"I think he's getting soft on us, Pete. What was it you were talking about the other day, Jim? Something about a sailboat and Italy and six months off?" Jim smiled, but inside he felt a stir of anger. It wasn't the teasing, because he never really took himself that seriously. But for Anita to share something so personal with Pete—who at the end of the day Jim thought was a scoundrel at worst and a social parasite at best—that was a problem for him. He would have to talk to Anita. Not only was it a personal betrayal of sorts, but she shouldn't say things like that to people for professional reasons. If they smelled blood, people in this business could be like sharks.

"Really!" Pete slapped Jim on the back. "Thinking about getting out of the game, huh? You *are* getting soft! Ha!" Pete laughed again. Jim wondered how many drinks Pete had had before arriving. "I never thought I'd see the day," Pete said, shaking his head and exchanging his empty flute glass for a full one as a waiter sashayed by.

Pete and Jim were in the same business, but the way they did business could not have been more different. Jim had always worked his tail off. Pete was a networker. He made connections and did the least work possible to garner the biggest fees he could squeeze from the deals he brokered. Jim was all about execution and a personal touch. Jim owned a mansion in the best part of town, and Pete had a townhouse he still couldn't pay off near, but not in, the swanky River Oaks subdivision. Pete looked the part, but Jim was the real deal. Jim pitied Pete in a way. He was single, had no kids, and for all intents and purposes, seemed to want to be Jim.

Jim suddenly spotted his oldest son, James, in the crowd, which was thickening by the minute. "If you'll excuse me, Peter." Jim was thankful for the excuse to extricate himself, and he was genuinely excited to see his son, which was more than he could say for the rest of the crowd.

"Of course, of course. I was just kidding you, Jim. You know that, right?"

Jim gave Pete a tight smile and headed toward James, whom they affectionately referred to as "JJ," for James Junior.

"Whoops," Jim heard Pete say to Anita as Jim walked away from the pair.

"I think you pissed him off," Anita said.

"Well, regardless, you look splendid tonight," Pete said as he looked Anita up and down, admiring her from top to bottom as she soaked up the adoration. She watched his eyes closely, as if in anticipation, and welcomed every minute of his flirt.

A moment passed as he took her in. "Be careful, Peter. Don't envy what you can't afford."

"Ah, but you are a Torino; you have plenty of money. But what *would* you do if the ol' boy hung up his shoes?" Pete asked with a big grin.

"Oh dear! That would put a hitch in my giddyup…now listen, be a champ and help me welcome all of these revelers."

Anita and Pete stood in the foyer of the splendid English Tudor mansion, working the crowd like a hand and glove, as if in a natural and unscripted dance.

Jim's momentary sympathy for Pete evaporated, and he made a mental note to kick Pete's ass all over the tennis court next time they played at the club.

The foyer spilled into a huge great room that was set off from a splendid kitchen. This room could easily sit twelve comfortably, but today, with four sets of French doors open, people were flowing into the yard. There, bartenders served everything from green apple martinis to Malbec, and any mixed drink you could muster. More than a hundred people were mingling about. To the left of the great room, there was a huge hearth and fireplace with an imported stone mantle. Above the mantle was a stunning oil of two men in English riding suits, one with a red coat and the other in black, each holding the reins of his steed. The riders were in a meadow as if taking a break from the day's foxhunt. As one scanned the room from left to right, eight double French doors looked over a manicured yard and pool. Tonight the pool glowed a royal blue, and a four-foot fountain of a boy on a sow in a playful pose poured water into the pool. The hog's head was stretched as if looking to the stars, and through its mouth a full stream of water arched up and into the pool. A boxwood hedge bordered the decking, cutting the pool off from the rest of the yard, which spread another forty feet beyond. Back in the corner was the playhouse and swing Jim and Anita's children had played on.

Neighbors, friends from the children's school years, and friendly business associates were at the party. The Swansons were well respected in the crowds they hung around. And for Anita, the invitation list reflected the family's popularity.

After shaking hands and visiting with guests, Jim finally made it across the room. "JJ!" Jim said, calling to his firstborn as he walked to the back of the house. Jim hadn't seen his son for at least six months. JJ was accompanied by his lovely, if a little cool, wife, Jane. They were young socialites in Houston. Jane, a private school teacher, spent many evenings and weekends volunteering for the Houston Junior League, while JJ worked long hours.

"Dad." James smiled at his father. "Happy birthday, old man!"

"Oh, it's like that, huh?" Jim said, shaking his head with mock hurt. Jim exchanged pleasantries with Jane before Anita appeared and took Jane's hand, leading her to the kitchen where they would conspire about Thanksgiving and Christmas and lock down the rest of the year's social calendar. Jim didn't mind. JJ was a runner, too, and Jim was eager to share his race results with him. Just as Jim was about to bring up the subject, ready to dispel any rumors that he indeed was becoming an old man, JJ stopped him.

"Is that Carson Tucker?" JJ nodded slightly toward an older man near where they were standing. Jim coughed under his breath and answered that it was. Carson was talking to Pete. "Can you make an introduction, Dad? He'd be perfect for the Daly deal we're working on."

JJ had followed in Jim's own footsteps and was an investment banking associate at the international investment banking firm Gorgan Brothers, specializing, like Jim, in mergers and acquisitions. Work in M&A, as the "street" called JJ's work, was prestigious and competitive. When Jim was young and getting started, he was just like his son: always on the lookout for the right hand shake, connecting, opening doors. You had to be. These jobs were extremely sought after, and someone was always right behind you, waiting to take your place if you blew a deal or lost focus.

"Come on, son. I'll make an introduction..." Jim paused. "But listen, let's spend some good time together soon." JJ looked at his father blankly, then laughed.

"Where's this coming from, Dad?" JJ's eyes tracked Tucker while he spoke, making sure he didn't lose him.

"I just think we should spend a little more...quality time together."

W"You getting sentimental in your old age, Dad?" JJ turned his attention to his father.

"Maybe I am, Son. Maybe I am." He smiled.

"Well, it might be the champagne talking, Pop. Let me know if you still want to play catch in the morning."

"Very funny. Come on. Let's go meet Carson."

Jim made introductions and then receded to the background. Carson was a billionaire who'd made his money consolidating and breaking apart companies and their components. His deals were so frequent that he knew every banker in town well. In fact, he probably worked harder than the investment bankers, which was why he'd burned three marriages and had little to show in terms of family. What he did have to show was his name, and it was everywhere. Multimillion-dollar gifts to hospitals, universities, museums—anywhere he could have his name plastered, it probably was. The recognition stroked his ego, which seemed to be incessantly in need of stroking.

"JJ, it's nice to meet you. I've always been an admirer of your father. It takes a lot to raise kids the way he's seemed to and be successful in his line of work. What do you do?"

"I'm in M&A at Gorgan Brothers. I work in Gabe McBrian's group," JJ said.

"Listen, I like McBrian, and we do some work together. But seriously, are you following in your father's footsteps, or is this is a stepping-stone to something else? I've got some advice for you," Tucker said.

"Well, uh, yeah. I mean, I'd love the advice."

"Listen, your dad is one of kind. If you stay in banking, do what he did: stay focused on your family and make it your priority. I see too many guys get started with bright ideas and big eyes and wake up empty-handed. That's why I've always liked your dad; he's one of the guys who seemed to keep his cards in order, if you know what I mean. He kept the priorities right, you know?"

JJ wanted to keep Carson talking as long as he could, but stumbled for a response. He took a second too long, and someone else approached the King Maker. As Tucker turned to shake hands, he said to JJ, "Nice meeting you...hey, how did your dad do in that triathlon today?"

"Uh..." was all JJ could get out before Tucker was pulled away.

Jim couldn't shake the heaviness of his mood, and his interactions with both JJ and Pete hadn't helped. He thought back to the days when JJ was like a puppy at his heels. A little boy with bangs hanging in his handsome young face and Jim's own big, light-blue eyes. Dammit. Jim felt like nine times out of ten, he had been too busy working to play. Hindsight truly was twenty-twenty. Was he getting to the age when he realized youth was truly wasted on the young?

When JJ was born, Jim and Anita had been living in a cramped one-bedroom apartment in Palo Alto while Jim finished his MBA at Stanford University. Anita was footing the bill, but his pride required they live modestly.

In the early 1980s, the Torinos' bank weathered the Texas bust better than most regional banks. When the state opened up banking to non-state-domiciled holding companies, the Torino family sold out for millions. Anita, along with her siblings and cousins, was set for life. While she'd never need to work a day in her life, Anita hadn't settled down with someone whose own career success was in question. Likewise for Jim, letting Anita support him for life was out of the question—he had his own clear ambition. Just as it had been for him in high school and college, he wasn't the brightest star in the class, but he worked his tail off at Stanford and got through it with respectable marks.

After business school, Jim landed a job in mergers and acquisitions in New York at First Boston. Being busy with his studies was quickly replaced by being 110 percent consumed with work. He soared through the ranks because he worked twice as hard as anyone else, and he was good. His instincts were sharp, and his people skills were even better. There were long hours, dinners, lunches, and golf on the weekends. He and Anita had two more children, Mary and Sarah. He loved them ferociously, but the work meant he rarely saw them. At the time, he had thought everything he was doing was for them. *All of them.* But now, looking back while watching them tonight at his fifty-fourth birthday party, he wasn't sure what it all had been for. Had he replayed a slightly different version of his own father's story? Sure, Jim had insane amounts of money, but just like his own father before him, he had let too many other commitments weigh on the relationships he had with his own children. Jim felt sick and stepped through the kitchen to the back stairwell that led upstairs to his bedroom. As he walked down the hallway to the master suite, he felt himself break out into a sweat.

The suite held two rooms in one. Sitting to one side, over-looking the pool and backyard and shaded by hundred-year-old live oaks, was a sitting area with a love seat and a comfortable but refined chair. They were angled together but shared a view of the flat-screen TV. Near the chair stood a tall lamp, which provided warm reading light, and across from both the sofa and the chair was an ottoman to make sitting, reading, or watching television relaxing. Across the room was a king-size bed with matching antique night tables. As Jim and Anita lay in bed, they could either see the glow of the pool to the left or the gas fireplace to the right. While the nights were not often cold, the Swansons loved to flip the fireplace on in the winter as they wound their evenings down. For Jim, he could look for hours at a flame, softening and slowing the problems of a transaction he was working on. The fire was therapy.

He made his way into the room and through the master bath to his space. He wiped his brow and approached the small island in the middle of his impressive walk-in closet. He kept his wallet, keys, and Blackberry on a tray on the island, surrounded by his vast array of suits and shoes. He rummaged in his slim wallet for a piece of paper. He couldn't think clearly and felt like he was going to pass out. He found what he was looking for, shoved it into the pocket of his slacks, and walked toward the bathroom.

He splashed water on his face and dried his neck with a hand towel.

"What the hell?" he said to himself, removing the slip of paper from his pocket. It was the pharmacy prescription. His doctor's illegible scrawl covered the small piece of paper. "*Am* I depressed?" Jim wondered aloud. He thought of the happiness, contentment, and excitement he'd felt just hours before at his race. Whatever it was, he was confused and obviously going through something. He had to get back to the party. He took a deep breath and shoved the piece of paper back into his pocket, as if its mere existence would serve as some sort of antidote to what was ailing him.

Jim got himself back together and rejoined the party. Sarah and Mary had arrived with their husbands, having left their young children home with babysitters. Both girls brushed his cheeks with perfunctory kisses. They squealed when they saw JJ and Jane. It was clear that the siblings were close, but Jim felt locked out. If so, it was his own fault. As he watched his kids animatedly catch up, he thought back to their childhoods in New York.

Things had been good with Anita in those days. She had nannies to help her with the kids, and she was the perfect Wall Street wife. She was smart and charming, and Jim was damn proud of her. Anita was happy, too. She surrounded herself with a crowd of like-minded Wall Street wives in the city. Her days were filled with tennis matches, lunches, shopping and play dates, and charity events. Anita leveraged New York's social opportunities like a pro. The contacts she made during that time set her up for a satisfying career in interior decorating later. But as parents, had they messed up? Irrevocably messed up? There was no getting that time back. Mary and Sarah, his little girls now grown up, had barely managed to wish him a happy birthday before they submerged themselves into the life of the party. Could he ever close this divide created by years of neglect? What had he been thinking?

By the time Anita had ushered the last guest out the door, Jim was in his pajamas and in bed. Anita came through their bedroom door, glassy-eyed and smiling like a cat that had just swallowed a canary.

"It was glorious. Everyone had a blast!" she said. She started toward him, seductively removing one stiletto at a time and tossing it aside casually. She unpinned her hair and let it spill over her shoulders as she let her dress fall to her feet, revealing the surprise of her lingerie. But Jim wasn't nearly as drunk as she was, and he was still angry with her.

"What was that all about with Pete?" Anita looked confused for a moment. She stepped out of her dress.

"What are you talking about? And why are we talking? Do you see what I'm wearing?" She was smiling and hoping to give herself as the icing on the cake of his birthday party.

"Anita, you can't tell people I'm thinking of taking a break. You know how people are in this business. If they sense any weakness or opportunity, they pounce." Her smile faded. She sat there for a few moments and then squinted and turned to the bathroom. She grabbed a robe from the closet, glaring at Jim as she returned, tying the belt around her waist.

"You can be a real asshole, Jim. I just threw you this huge party, dressed up for you"—she waved her hand across her body—"and this is what I get in return? What is wrong with you?"

"I don't know," Jim said. But they were talking about two different things, and he knew it. "Look, you're right. Thank you. It was a beautiful party, and you did an excellent job. I just...you can't do that, Anita. You can't talk to people like that."

"Got it." She went to the bathroom and slammed the door.

Jim was worn out. He'd fix things in the morning.

FOUR

Jim loved Monday mornings. For some, it was the end of the fun, but for Jim, it meant the fun was just beginning. He loved routine. It's what got him going at five o'clock in the morning, when the sharp chirp of the alarm clock pierced the heavy silence of sleep and darkness. A morning run through the quiet streets of his affluent neighborhood would precede the real heat and humidity of the days in Houston. He loved watching lights pop on. They reminded him of sudden ideas as he streamed past the large, opulent houses and manicured lawns of his neighbors. Some were quietly padding out their front doors in bathrobes to retrieve their newspapers, a habit that would surely be extinct soon thanks to Steve Jobs and Apple. Jim himself would read three newspapers on his iPad after his run while he downed a light breakfast of scrambled egg whites and coffee before heading into the office. As CEO of his own investment-banking firm, he answered to no one, but being a good boss was important to him, and being disciplined and habitual ran deep in his DNA. He was always at his desk by eight thirty.

This Monday morning in particular came as a relief to Jim. He needed to get out of the house and back to work. While he worked his way through his morning routine, he felt the uneasy feelings of the weekend slip away. Once again, he chalked them up to an odd mood as he slipped into the Mercedes CLS. He traveled his well-worn route to work. The car was a dream, and its formidable tires smoothed the ride down Main Street as he passed near a source of Houston's pride—the august acres of Rice University and Houston's esteemed medical center.

"How was it?" Jim's secretary of fifteen years, Coco Young, peered up at him over her signature heavy-rimmed black glasses. Her thick hair, blond and lined with gray, fell just past her shoulders. Anita would say it was too long for her age.

"The party?" Jim asked, suddenly feeling guilty and awkward that Anita had not extended an invitation to Coco.

"Oh, yes, of course. I'd love to know how the party was, but I meant the race." Coco raised her eyebrows with a knowing look. Jim clapped his hands together, forgetting himself.

"Pretty fantastic!" he said enthusiastically.

"Time?"

"One fifty-six!...well, one fifty-six thirty-one...but the thirty-one seconds don't count, right?"

"Really?" Coco asked with a delicious combination of both admiration and surprise in her voice. Jim felt himself well up with pride beneath the fine wool of his suit jacket. She scooted him into his office with updates and coffee and left Jim feeling like a million bucks. He watched her go as she headed back to her desk. She was attractive, but she hid herself beneath matronly clothing that was too big and left her looking a bit shapeless. He let himself wonder for a moment what Coco would look like outfitted in one of Anita's tailored suits. He felt a slight stir and coughed to shake the image. He shook his head and dove into the day's work.

The morning flew by as he put out fires and offered guidance to the young, hungry flock that made up his deal team.

After a quick lunch at his desk, Coco came in and said Pete Matli was requesting dinner that evening at Cristo's. Apparently he had a deal he wanted to discuss with Jim. Pete worked at a smaller bank and occasionally referred deals that were a better fit for those who would do the work. Jim wasn't dying to have dinner with Pete, but he accepted the invitation. This was business.

Cristo's was a high-end restaurant located between two of Houston's affluent enclaves, River Oaks and West University Place, and owned by one of Houston's notable restauranteurs. On any given night, the place was packed with not only well-heeled CEOs like Jim, but also writers, artists, oil barons, and society mavens.

When Jim arrived, Pete was already seated, and Jim noticed that he had taken the liberty of ordering a bottle of wine for the table. The two men greeted each other with a hearty handshake, and Jim sat down. His first thought, as it often was at a swanky place, was a wish that he could remove his jacket. But at Cristo's, you either came in a $500-golf shirt, impeccably pressed slacks, and driving loafers, or you kept your jacket on. The bottle meant they had something significant to talk about.

When they finished the business of ordering dinner, Jim squinted his blue eyes. "So you got me here, Matli. What's up?"

"Great party the other night."

Jim nodded in response. "That's all Anita. Can't take any credit there."

"You're a lucky man, Jim," Pete said, taking a sip of his sparkling water.

"In many ways, indeed...you have me there..." Jim didn't want to discuss Anita with Pete.

"Yes. Listen, Jim. I've got an interesting deal out of Argentina for your firm. It's a big fish, a little too big for our shop."

"I like the sound of that," Jim said, sipping his wine and turning the bottle around to look at its label. "Malbec? It's great. Interesting choice."

"Apt choice. Remember, the company I want to talk to you about is based in Argentina," Pete said. He was smiling.

"Ah," Jim said, understanding Pete's wine pick and chuckling in return. The Malbec grape hailed from Argentina. "Do tell."

"Look, Jim, I've been contacted by a customer of an old client who owns one of Latin America's largest oil and gas equipment manufacturers. The business makes the full suite of equipment: they make tubing, valves, rams, compressors, and other components needed for exploration and production operators. The company has many patents, but two are especially promising. One could be used to enhance production of fracking operations, which, as you know, is an area that has exploded in the United States. The other is a fail-safe solution that, from what I understand, could have prevented the Macondo well explosion in the Gulf of Mexico in 2010." Pete paused.

"I'm with you." Jim nodded as a signal for Pete to continue while his mind raced to figure out which company it might be.

"This business is doing $450 million in worldwide sales, mostly in South America. The investment banking firm Klyner Peabody has been shopping the idea of taking them out and getting some interest. With low interest rates and cash pouring in due to high oil prices, corporations are looking to grow through acquisitions. I'm not telling you anything you don't know here."

"Where do I come in?"

"Well, this isn't our kind of deal. I definitely want to send it your way, but there's a caveat."

"OK. What is it?" Jim asked plainly. Two servers arrived with their entrées, placing them simultaneously while Jim waited for Pete to answer. While listening, he was also relishing the majesty of the square plate set in front of him. He'd ordered Tasmanian Salmon Vignole—seared Tasmanian salmon with Meyer lemons, fava beans, peas, and artichokes.

"Normally I'd tell you to just send your best guy, but this is different. The owner of the business, a man named Jose Carlo Segrato, has built this business from the ground up."

"Attached," Jim said knowingly before taking a bite of his fish. The salmon was cooked medium rare to 140 degrees in the center, which, when done right by Tony Vallone, equaled perfection.

"To say the least," Pete said.

Jim thought this over for a minute as he took a sip of wine. It was easy for a CEO who'd risen through the ranks of an existing company to sell it. Those sorts of CEOs: guys out of Harvard and Wharton, *institutional managers*, saw the operating and selling of businesses as one and the same. The end game was to return the most profit to shareholders and to walk with a package large enough to ride the golden parachute to a life where work became optional.

"You've got to go yourself, Jim. It's the only way. This guy is sixty-eight and old school."

Jim studied Pete for a moment. The guy could be an ass at times, but he did have good instincts. "Buenos Aires?" Jim asked. He was a fan of the city. Tango, steak, and wine: what was not to like? That said, the country was a mess, politically and economically. But Pete was right. Normally, Jim would send one of his best people. He hadn't had to handhold a deal himself in nearly a decade. But the timing might be just right. He thought about the disconnect that he was feeling lately with Anita and that strange murky feeling that kept coming over him at home. A little trip might be just what the doctor ordered.

On his drive home, Jim thought about what Pete had told him about this Jose Carlo Segrato character. Sixty-eight years old.

Jim shook his head. This man had started making pipe fittings in a warehouse forty-four years ago. He started with nothing, and through blood, sweat, and tears had founded and built a company with eight hundred employees in nine countries.

Jim felt for this man. Owners like this were more than married to their companies. They *were* their companies. Sometimes the company was the alter ego of the man, like Bill Gates and Microsoft, and other times the man was the alter ego of the company, like Apple and Steve Jobs. Either way, these relationships didn't end easily.

What's more, the last thing a man like Jose Carlo would care to hear about was his company being sliced and diced in purely monetary terms. Jim imagined a team of Klyner Peabody bankers opining about the multiples that could be earned on $75 million in earnings before interest, taxes, depreciation, and amortization (EBITDA). What founders would want to see a bunch of whipper-snappers salivating, practically holding up their knives and forks, ready to carve into their life's work? Things could get really hot when these characters started talking about leveraging cash flows by adding mountains of debt to juice returns and maybe let the owner pull some cash out. These guys would lose their credibility on the spot. No one could run a company for forty-four years without a few close calls, and Jim was certain Jose Carlo's company was no different. Debt was no friend; it was to be feared.

Jim pressed the button to turn off the car's ignition. He sat in the strange half-light of their four-car garage for a moment. The same heavy feeling he had left behind this morning returned. He slipped off his tie and took a deep breath. He drummed his fingers on the steering wheel, grabbed his briefcase, and headed into the house.

FIVE

"Hey, sleepy head." Marco heard his mother's gentle voice tunneling through his dreams amid the sounds of metallic and gravel churning out from the rail yard across the road from their housing project. His eyelids felt heavy, but his feet were sticking out of the thin covers, and he was cold. It was September, which here in the Southern Hemisphere meant winter was loosening its hold, but there was still a chill in the air. Waking up and getting warm might not be the worst thing. Magdalena ran her hands lovingly through Marco's thick, black hair. She took his feet in her hands and began to rub them, singing a little song as she did.

In another part of the room, Marco's aunt was frying something—it didn't smell good. He would wait and eat something at the church. Today was Saturday, and he had lessons with Father Diaz while his mother cleaned the chapel. Saturday was his favorite day. He got to be with his mother all day on Saturdays. The rest of the week he stayed at Villa Thirty-One with his aunt and cousins while his mother took the bus downtown, where she spent the mornings doing laundry in a large hotel and the evenings cleaning office buildings.

Villa Thirty-One was one of many slums, or shantytowns, in Buenos Aires. It was a system of ramshackle structures made of wood, tin, or whatever else its desperate inhabitants might be able to lay their hands on. The makeshift communities were connected by narrow, mazelike, dirt paths and home to peasants, criminals, prostitutes, and those from more rural parts of Argentina hoping to make better lives for themselves and those they left behind.

Marco's apartment was not unlike others in Villa Thirty-One. They had two rooms and a crude toilet, but no shower. Marco and his mother shared a thin mattress on the floor of the main room. The main room also served as a makeshift kitchen with a hot plate and a small pantry. The pantry was usually painfully bare as they lived hand-to-mouth, subsisting on whatever Magdalena could provide day-to-day—some fruit, chips, or pig rinds, potatoes, an onion or tomato, and maybe, if they had enough money to spare, nuts. Magdalena managed to provide enough for her sister to cook one meal a day for all of them.

There was one light in each room, and the main room contained a decrepit, old sofa beside Marco and Magdalena's bed. They used a box for a side table, and propped on the box was a framed photo of Marco and his mother. They were caught smiling and laughing in the park on a stunning spring afternoon—a good day. That photograph was a treasure to both of them. They had nothing else like it. It was the only thing in the flat that wasn't purely utilitarian.

Rosa, Marco's aunt, called him over to the hot plate to offer him some of the hideous thing she was cooking. He truly loved Saturdays. Marco tried to put Rosa off by telling her he had a stomachache, which could have been the truth. He had a very weak stomach. But Rosa wrinkled her nose at him and called him a *chiqueado* (brat). Marco's older cousin, Jorge, laughed, but Marco just ignored them. Jorge would spend the day playing soccer and getting in and out of all sorts of trouble. This wasn't really Jorge's fault. There was no schooling in the housing project, and children had to fend for themselves, unsupervised most of the time. Jorge was twelve—only two years older than Marco—but he was already developing a certain callousness that came with growing up in such a rough and unpredictable environment.

Magdalena noticed this new edge in Jorge, too, and worried for Marco. Oh, how she worried for Marco. She had grown up in the shantytown and was seduced into drug use and then forced into prostitution at a young age. When she became pregnant with Marco, she turned her life around by a rare combination of circumstance and will. She got clean and found a good job at a hotel. This sort of turnaround was unheard of. And it was just the beginning. Magdalena wanted out. She was determined to secure a better life for herself and Marco. So far she was doing a pretty good job. Marco was ten years old and had learned to read during his Saturday sessions with Father Diaz. But Jorge was a warning sign. Life in this *villa miseria* was a ticking time bomb. She had to get them out.

Magdalena kissed Rosa on the cheek, but Rosa only scowled and shoved her off. Rosa's twin toddlers, Sergio and Carla, swarmed around her legs, and Jorge left the flat without a word. Magdalena sighed. "Come on, *Mijo*. We are going to be late."

Marco and Magdalena wound their way through the odd collection of haphazard structures that made up Villa Thirty-One. The slum was next to a rail yard, just twenty meters from Avenida Leopoldo Lugones and not far from the Estadio Monumental on the banks of the Río de la Plata. As they passed a group of kids playing *fútbol*, Marco watched them. Every single one of those kids dreamed of playing for Argentina's national fútbol team. Magdalena followed Marco's eyes. She shook her head.

"No, no, Mijo. Keep your head in the books."

Marco nodded. "Si, *Mamá*," he said.

"Do you have your book, Marco?" Magdalena suddenly gasped. She seemed panicked.

"Si, Mamá." Marco laughed. He pulled a well-worn copy of *The Screwtape Letters* from beneath his shirt. He didn't like Jorge to see the books the father lent him. Jorge and Rosa did not know that Marco was studying with Father Diaz. It would have caused jealousy and trouble.

Magdalena had made a deal with the parish priest. She would spend Saturdays cleaning the church, and all she asked in return was that the father spend time tutoring Marco. Father Diaz was the real deal. He cared deeply for the people in his poor parish and obliged. He invited other families to join in, hoping to give the boys and girls in the community any skills that might give them a leg up. But few were there consistently. Marco, however, never missed, a credit to both him and Magdalena.

Marco stepped off the bus and as usual felt as if he were stepping into another world altogether. The church Marco's mother cleaned was located in Belgrano, one of Argentina's middle-class neighborhoods. While the parish itself was poor, it was a stone's throw from a fairly well-to-do *barrio*.

Their stop was Avenida Cabildo. They stepped off the bus and onto the busy avenue. Always bustling, the street roared with life on the weekends. *La Capilla*, as locals called the church, lay off a small side street at the end of the lively Avenida Cabildo. Marco always felt as if there were a heavy piece of glass between him and the strangers he observed on this weekly walk toward the church. His world was so different from theirs. People lingered at outdoor cafes, their plates arriving in front of them with food steaming and hot. Cups of coffee, jars of fresh flowers. High-heeled shoes and big, dark sunglasses.

They walked at a fast clip, but Marco always stopped to look up at the movie theater marquee. Naturally, no one he knew owned a *tele*, but he saw them playing here and there. Shop owners usually kept one perched above their cash registers—more often than not, a fútbol match was on. But the marquee of the theater and the idea of a movie truly captivated him. His mother promised that they would go one day when he was older. She had never been herself.

Father Diaz was in his office when Marco and his mother arrived. He was a short portly man with a heavy, graying beard. His face was round, and he had red cheeks. He wore black with the distinctive white collar of his vocation. Hanging from his neck was a large chain and a crucifix. His stomach rounded over his belt. He was not heavy from good food and an abundant lifestyle. His heft came from a tireless devotion to ministry. He sacrificed exercise and activity for engaging with and relating to those whom he could serve, often visiting the homes of the ill or grieving or staying long hours at the hospital, praying with the dying.

"*Has comido?*" he asked as a greeting. Marco shook his head. Magdalena blushed with shame. "I saved something for you both." Father nodded to a tray of *medialunas—pasteles* always filled with something surprising and delicious—and two cups of *café con leche*. The croissants were fluffy and obviously baked that morning. The women who cooked for the parish were excellent cooks and made magic with meager supplies. Marco broke into a big grin that was contagious. Magdalena and Father Diaz laughed.

"I am going to get to work, Mijo. Be good."

"Magdalena, can you clean the organ today?"

"Of course!" Magdalena said.

"And then I must insist that you join us for lunch when you are finished with your work."

"*Gracias, Padre.*" Magdalena ducked out of the room.

39

Father Diaz turned to Marco. "So, are you ready to get down to business?" Marco nodded. "Tell me, what do you think of old Screwtape and Wormwood?" Marco frowned in response, anxious that his answer would not please Father Diaz. He had found the story unnerving and disturbing, but he was a courageous soul and always spoke the truth to the priest.

"Wormwood and Screwtape seem to be mean. They just want the patient to harm and hurt others. Why would someone write such an awful story?" he finally said. Father Diaz laughed in response. Marco sucked in his breath. Had he said something stupid?

"My child, very good!" the priest said, and Marco let out a sigh of relief. "The writer was a great believer and was devoted in all ways to his faith in God and our Lord Jesus Christ. But he knew he had to be clever in order cast his message wide." Marco looked a bit confused.

Father Diaz switched tack. "What he wanted us to learn from the story is that the devil is quite real. He also wanted us to see how the devil might manipulate us into doing wrong, manipulate us into going against our better judgment." Marco listened. Father Diaz posed a simple question. "What does Screwtape want, Marco?"

Marco pondered the question. "Well, he is sneaky. He tries to lead others to do exactly what they shouldn't. He also gets them to do what they don't want to do. This is what makes him happy," he finally said.

"Very good, Marco. Exactly."

"But how can he be happy to see others do such bad things? That's what I don't understand."

"But perhaps you do. Don't you think he wants us to do wrong? After all, his boss is the Father Below. And we both know who that is," said the priest.

"Satan. Not a good boss." Both Father and Marco laughed.

"My boss is Jesus, the one and only true God. As you grow up, Marco, you will see—or perhaps you are already seeing—that some people help us to do good, and others want to lead us down a path of sin," Father Diaz said in a sober tone. Marco thought of Jorge.

"Wormwood and Screwtape will fool people and lead them toward evil," Marco said, nodding his head with genuine understanding.

"Exactly."

"And in life, you don't always know whether someone is going to help you be a good person or a bad person." Marco sat silently for a long time and again thought of Jorge, who was surrounded by forces that wanted him to be bad, to fail. And now Jorge himself was becoming a force for bad instead of good. Marco wondered if he might help his cousin in some way.

"Padre, there is something I don't understand," Marco said, breaking the silence. "There is a chapter where Screwtape is talking about humans. He says something about the law of undulation. What does that mean?"

"Read it to me, child."

Marco fumbled through the pages, finding the section in chapter eight.

"My dear Wormwood..." Marco read slowly and carefully, and became more focused as he continued. "As long as he lives on earth, periods of emotional and bodily richness and liveliness will alternate with periods of numbness and poverty. The dryness and dullness through which your patient is now going are not, as you fondly suppose, your workmanship; they are merely a natural phenomenon which will do us no good unless you make a good use of it."[1]

---

1   C. S. Lewis, *The Screwtape Letters*, rev. ed. (New York: Macmillan Publishing Company, 1982), 37.

"This is what I do not understand." Marco sighed.

With this Father Diaz shot up! He was excited and happy and reached for the boy with a great big hug. "*Niño*! You are so bright! I am very, very proud of you."

Marco was nestled in the hug, but he was confused. As Father Diaz pulled away, he looked at the boy and realized he did not understand the priest's excitement.

"Ah, My Child, let me explain. First, we must understand what is meant by *undulation*. It is a very big word with a very deep meaning as it is used here. It means to go up and down, like a... uh...uh...like a Ferris wheel. It goes up and down. But the author is describing how our lives go up and down. Some days we are happy, and other days we are sad. Some things happen to us that bring us success, and other things come that bring us struggle or failure. Life is not always easy. Mr. Lewis, the author, is saying that this has nothing to do with God or with Satan. He is saying it was a part of how God made us. He made us so that we would have challenges as a part of our natural life journey. In our journey, some things would cause us to feel at the bottom, and other things, at the top. Did you read the rest of the chapter?"

Marco nodded.

"Good, read it again. You will see that Screwtape explains that God did this to give us the opportunity to demonstrate our faith in Him, and Him alone, during the difficult times. This is what Screwtape warns Wormwood about. He says, 'You need to be careful because when a person chooses to be faithful even in hardship, their faith is strengthened and they are less likely to fall,' as demons desire.

"My boy, there is another thing, too. I believe that what is greatest in humanity, what is greatest in our lives, is often defined by what we do when we are down, when things have gone badly.

For if we are going to remain faithful, God will show us great blessings. But more importantly, He will give us great opportunity to be a blessing to others. Some of the greatest things ever done in history were done because people chose the 'law of undulation' in their worst moments, chose to do what is right and to carry on and to respond."

Now Marco was wide-eyed, processing what the priest had shared but also smiling. He understood the chapter now. He could see that while it was difficult, people could overcome that which oppressed them rather than being defined by their struggles.

"As I said, Niño, I am proud of you. We have covered a lot today! You go outside and play now."

After lunch, Marco played in the sanctuary and in the small yard of the church, while his mother finished cleaning Father Diaz's apartment. When she was done, the women in the kitchen gave them a bag of the food containing all they could spare. Marco and Magdalena walked back to the bus stop hand-in-hand. Their hearts were filled with good feelings and joy. It had been a good day. They didn't have a lot in life, but they had each other, and that was more valuable than gold.

SIX

Jim was up to his elbows in raw meat and having the time of his life helping to prepare a feast in honor of his visit to the Segratos' vineyard.

"You're doing great, Jim!" said Jose Carlo's daughter, Anabella, in a rich, heavy Spanish accent. Jim smiled as he worked with a crew of men, two of whom were Jose Carlo's sons, to sort different cuts of beef. Jose Carlo, dressed in a light-cream, cable-knit sweater and cream slacks, watched from a patio that overlooked the vineyard and the farm where Jim and the men worked. Jim stuck up a gloved arm and waved. Jose Carlo nodded with approval. Anabella, who was a painter and ran the vineyard, was working nearby at a table, rolling and pinching dough for empanadas.

Jim had landed at Ministro Pistarini International Airport, fourteen miles southwest of Buenos Aires, the evening before and was immediately escorted to a smaller terminal, where he boarded the Segratos' private jet. The small aircraft carried him another two hours to the Mendoza region where the Segrato family ran a vineyard and small farm.

Jose Carlo had sent his car for Jim, which drove him from small El Plumerillo Airport thirty miles to the Segratos' vineyard. The driver had been chatty, and Jim was exhausted from the two flights. He had just wanted to close his eyes. It was the middle of the night, but the man was proud of his country and had a lot to say.

"Argentina is an incredible country, but she could be better! We have many resources, and we are big like your United States! We have mountain ranges more beautiful than any in the world." Jim nodded and smiled from the back seat. He tilted his head back. It was dark, and all he could see outside of the window was black. They had quickly left the lights of the airport behind and entered rural territory. "We offer skiing, climbing, and sightseeing. You Americans love us!" the driver said. Jim thought he spoke like an advertisement for Argentina. A true patriot.

The man, whose name Jim learned was Hector, took Jim's silence as an invitation to continue speaking. Jim figured they only had about thirty minutes. Either Hector would wind down, or they'd reach their destination. Jim was in no mood for conversation after a day of travel. "We get a bad story. Is that how you say it in English?"

"Bad rap," Jim said. Hector laughed, and Jim smiled. This was one happy guy.

"Yes, bad rap. There is corruption here, and our big sister Brazil gets more attention and does better. It is hard for the poor here, *Señor*. Very hard."

"One might say it is hard for poor people everywhere. Not an easy life."

"Yes, but in America, I know anyone thinks they can be anything. No? Like, Hector can be president if he tries." Hector took one hand off the wheel and slapped his thin chest. This made Jim laugh. He knew what Hector meant and conceded his point. He was tired and wasn't going to engage in any serious debate. "Here, I think people have lost hope. There is little motivation to work hard and be better. Not in America, sí? Pull yourself up! Right?"

Hector and Jim settled into silence, and Jim drifted off. When they arrived at the vineyard, Hector woke Jim and led him into the vineyard's formidable lobby, where a woman named Alisa was waiting for him. Alisa introduced herself as the Segratos' head housekeeper and led Jim to his room. Alisa told Jim that Jose Carlo and his family were looking forward to meeting Jim in the morning.

The room was elegant and masculine, which Jim admired. There was a large four-poster bed made from Brazilian the walnut wood that was so popular in Argentine design and furniture. A thick, colorful rug covered the red square tiles of the floor, and the room's walls were decorated in beautiful landscape paintings. Jim changed into his pajamas and poured into the inviting goose down of the bed. He was asleep in less than a minute.

In the morning, Jim finally met Jose Carlo face-to-face. Jim had slept late and showered and shaved quickly upon waking. He dressed and left his room, not quite sure where to go. It was a large property, but he followed the sound of voices. The Segrato family was gathered around a giant table when Jim entered the dining room. There were newspapers and empty coffee cups scattered about, and the room was full of the sort of unintelligible buzz that is created by several conversations being carried on at once. When they noticed Jim standing there, the room suddenly fell silent. A very attractive, well-dressed woman in her late sixties, whom Jim instantly assumed was Jose Carlo's wife, rose and offered Jim her hand.

"Mr. Swanson." She smiled. "I am Cecilia, Jose Carlo's wife."

"Please excuse me for not getting up, Jim. I have a bad knee that has been giving me a great deal of trouble these last few weeks," Jose Carlo said from the far end of the table. Out of respect, Jim shook Cecilia's hand warmly and quickly went to offer his hand to Jose Carlo.

"Señor Segrato, it is my pleasure. Our friend spoke highly of you and said that you needed help. We've been looking at the documents you've sent us, and I think we have a lot of good things to speak about," Jim said.

"Our friend is all business!" Jose Carlo said.

Jim laughed. "I am delighted to be here, Jose Carlo, Cecilia. Thank you for having me."

"We cannot take all of the credit, Jim." Jose Carlo held a beautiful hand-carved walking stick despite the fact that he was seated. He had a handsome, hawkish face. His skin was a rich shade of brown and deeply distinguished. "I must introduce you to my three children."

"Wonderful," Jim said, turning his attention back toward the crowd at the table. Jim was introduced to Anabella first. She ran the vineyard and lived on the property with her husband and two young children. The paintings in the room, as well as those Jim would later see that decorated the whole of the compound, were by her hand. A gifted artist, Jim wondered if she sold or exhibited them elsewhere. "She wouldn't be driven by any monetary need," Jim thought to himself.

Jose Carlo's sons, Roberto and Adolfo, had gathered for the occasion as well. Roberto, Jose Carlo's oldest, was in his early forties and a cardiologist. Adolfo was a university professor. The two men lived with their wives and children in an upscale neighborhood in Buenos Aires.

Cecilia explained to Jim that they had a fun and busy day planned for him. They hoped he was game. Jim dawned an expression of mock fear, and the Segrato clan laughed.

"Don't worry, Jim. I won't let them hurt you," Jose Carlo said in his commanding voice. Jim sighed with relief. "Well, not too much," Jose Carlo said with a smile.

Jim was served a small breakfast of pastries and coffee. He was told there would be a feast later and that he might want to save his appetite. Jim wondered whether he might get out for a run at some point or whether that would be considered rude. He would get to know them a bit more and decide.

Jim helped Jose Carlo out of his chair as everyone began to clear the room. "Let's have a chat, Jim," Jose Carlo said, leading Jim through large French doors that led to a veranda overlooking the property. Jim gasped. It was gorgeous. Rows and rows of grapes reached as far as the eye could see. The neat, manicured lines of grapes were met by the Andes, imposing and snow-capped. The sky was bright blue, and the air cool and arid.

Jose Carlo, obviously immune to the view, ignored Jim's reaction. "You are probably wondering why I've made you come all this way."

"The thought crossed my mind," Jim said in a friendly tone. He had indeed wondered, but had figured there were worse ways to spend a few days than working on a deal at a vineyard that grew the Malbec grape. He was well-traveled and pretty at ease in any environment. He may have been curious, but he wasn't fazed.

"Jim, my parents came from Italy. They immigrated to Buenos Aires with my family, my father's sister, and her son. My father was a welder and taught both of us boys, my cousin and myself, to work hard and make something of ourselves. And we were smart to follow his advice." Jose Carlo nodded to the expanse of land that lay in front of them. "Sí?"

"Sí," Jim said.

"My cousin and I—his name was Luca—started a company in La Boca, a very industrial part of Buenos Aires. Somewhere I am sure you will never have a reason to go, Jim." Jim nodded. "Anyway, Luca later died of cancer, leaving two daughters, my nieces."

"I'm sorry for your loss."

"It was a long time ago, but thank you." Jose Carlo produced a thin gold cigarette case from the pocket of his fine, cream-colored trousers. He offered one to Jim, but Jim smiled and shook his head. "It's a terrible habit, but one must have a vice."

"Certainly," Jim agreed. He was mostly staying quiet. He knew Jose Carlo wanted a good listener, and Jim had that skill to offer. There would be a time to talk, but now was not that time. Jose Carlo obviously wanted to share his story. As if reading Jim's mind, Jose Carlo blew out a plume of smoke and looked at Jim plainly.

"You have an expression in America. It's not personal; it's business. Do you agree with this sentiment?"

"At times." Jim answered honestly.

"You are smart. I have dealt with Americans over the years and people from many other countries: you would lose your hide if you didn't think that way. But for me, here in Argentina, here on this land, here with my family, it is very personal."

"I understand, Jose Carlo. Please tell me more about yourself." Jim noticed an ashtray at a nearby table and placed it beneath the growing ash of Jose Carlo's cigarette.

"Gracias," Jose Carlo said, tipping his cigarette. Jim began to take the ashtray away, but Jose Carlo waved him back. He stubbed out his cigarette. "It is a nasty habit indeed. Come on, let's walk. It hurts like a, how do you say, a...uh..."

"I get it...a lot!" Jim said.

"Sí, but it's worse if I don't move it," Jose Carlo said, referring to his bad knee.

The two men strolled through the lush grounds of the vineyard and the small farm that sat adjacent to the rows and rows of grapes.

Jose Carlo explained that running an oil field supply company was a dirty business. When his kids were young, Jose Carlo had spent long hours at the warehouse while Cecilia raised their children. Jim could certainly relate to that part of the story and said as much. As the company grew, Jose Carlo moved his family out of La Boca and eventually to Palermo, where they lived in a mansion built by a cattle baron in the early nineteen hundreds. The house felt too big now that the children had grown. He and Cecilia came to the vineyard as much as they could these days to see their grandchildren.

As Jim and Jose Carlo turned back toward the house, Jose Carlo stopped suddenly. "You are a good listener, Jim." The two men laughed.

"Please, Jose Carlo, it's the reason I am here. You have my ear. Take your time."

Jose Carlo continued to share stories about how he'd arrived at this point and why he was, for the first time in his long career, listening to ideas about selling his enterprise. He shared how much he cared for and loved his employees, giving them credit for much of the hard work. He also commented on his children and their interests. Jim could hear sincere pride in what Jose Carlo had created with the help of many people, and yet there was a realization, as Jose Carlo limped along, that perhaps he was seeing his stamina decline. Jose Carlo was trying to determine what that meant to the company.

By the time the two men parted back at the house, Jim had learned a lot about Jose Carlo as a man and about his company.

Jim wasn't expected anywhere for two hours, so he changed into his running clothes and darted back through the vineyards. It felt great to stretch his legs. The bright, cool day was perfect. As he increased his speed, taking in the smells and sights around him, he thought about what he'd learned.

In the past decade, several forces had joined together to put Jose Carlo's company in an exceptional position.

As developing countries of South America were emerging, energy exploration was expanding. Then, a supercycle in oil began driving prices from twenty dollars a barrel to over a hundred. As a result, it was more economical to drill in many new locations. Demand was climbing, and many believed oil production had reached a peak. This meant that supply would begin a sharp decline while demand would continue to grow at an exponential rate.

To add to this, new technologies were being developed to help companies move into older wells and accelerate the production levels considerably. When these late-life properties were about to be shut down by major producers, smaller producers, who often bought the properties cheaply, could employ these new technologies. Increased production was not what helped Jose Carlo. It was the fact that this increased production did not last long. So after a few years, the rigs had to be moved. Moving a rig to begin drilling in a new location required a lot of component upgrades, as well as new components depending on the geological formation in which the rig was being placed.

This oil supercycle and the new technologies used on older wells meant that a client's orders might double *and* that the client might come back for new stock each year instead of every three or four. These factors had taken Jose Carlo's company from about $80 million in sales to $750 million. Jose Carlo and his team had been able to manage the growth well. They had little debt and decent margins. They were considered a reliable provider, and often customers sought their design assistance, which earned a higher margin for Jose Carlo but was also a critical service for the client.

With an artist, a cardiologist, and a professor as children, none of Jose Carlo's descendants were going to step into his shoes. He didn't want them to, either. With Klyner Peabody calling, he was seriously listening.

But Jose Carlo also knew he needed help. He was smart and read people well. But this was the most important opportunity he'd ever encountered. If he did this right, his family would be one of Argentina's ruling elite for many generations to come. Jose Carlo had shared with Jim that perhaps he'd even have a grandson who'd become a senator.

After Jose Carlo was referred to Pete Matli, Jim's name had surfaced as someone who might be able help. Jose Carlo had heard that Jim was no-nonsense. A good friend of Jose Carlo's had been looking at the sale of his soybean business, and Jim had talked him out of it. He'd said that the family was too tied to the business and that any one of the owner's children would be able to run the company in a heartbeat. While Jim had agreed that the offer price was reasonable, he'd felt that the company could expand into Brazil and that if they were successful, the enterprise would be worth three or four times more. The soybean family loved Jim and trusted him implicitly.

Now Jim was sorting different cuts of beef, helping prepare for the night's feast. "Where are you, Jim?" Roberto, Jose Carlo's son, was smiling and looking at Jim.

"I was thinking about your father," Jim said honestly.

"Ah The patriarch!" Adolfo said with admiration.

"Our work is done here, Jim." Jim looked down. He had been so deep in thought that he had shifted into autopilot. The beef sat in sorted heaps in front of the men.

"Go get cleaned up. Take your time. When the sun begins to set, we will feast!" the two men said.

"That was really fun, fellas," Jim said. He had milked a cow, sorted beef, and made cheese in the hours since his run. It had been an incredible day. His troubles felt far away and like another man's altogether.

That night they dined beneath a sky riddled with stars. There were steaming cups of yerba maté and empanadas filled with onion, egg, spinach, pork, beef, and cheese. The table was finished with some of the best wine Jim had ever enjoyed, and the splendid setting and welcoming company enriched the meal. Tomorrow he would accompany Jose Carlo back to Buenos Aires where they would discuss the terms of the deal. But for tonight, Jim just relaxed and enjoyed himself. Topping off the night was Jose Carlo playing a mean acoustic guitar accompanied by his two sons. Jim was struck by this and wished he could experience this type of camaraderie with his own children. He also felt like he could repeat this very same day every day for a year before he tired of any of it. He wondered how he could take something of the experience and apply it to his life back in Houston. He would have to find a way to capture some of the magic of pastoral Argentina.

"The amazing thing about your Malbec grape is that it holds the same body and complexity as the big Cabernets from California or the Bordeaux from France, but its tannins are so much softer. I could drink this red wine all day long," Jim said as the family all nodded with grins of agreement.

SEVEN

Magdalena stood in the middle of the flat, thinking. Rosa was in the bathroom with her head against the toilet. Jorge and the twins were in bed, green-faced and recovering from a night of vomit and discomfort. Somehow Marco and Magdalena had been spared the stomach bug that had invaded their flat. Magdalena wanted to stay and take care of her sister, but she couldn't. If she missed another day of work, there might be trouble; already she had missed three days due to another illness earlier in the year. Magdalena feared that leaving Marco at home would just infect him, so she decided to take him along for the day, hoping things would be OK.

"Marco, you are coming with Mamá today," she said. Marco looked up. He was drawing with the stub of a pencil on the back of a cardboard box he'd found the day before. He smiled.

"*Bueno*, Mamá!" Magdalena wasn't sure what she was going to do with him all day while she worked, but she simply couldn't leave him here.

"Jorge." Magdalena looked at her nephew with seriousness. "You need to take care of the twins today and your mamá." Jorge wasn't feeling too hot, but he nodded. "Swear to me, Jorge."

"I swear, *Tía*." Jorge had a sweet side, and Magdalena was depending on it today. Magdalena approached Rosa with a cool washcloth, but Rosa waved her away. "Get out of here, Magdalena. You don't want this."

The people at the hotel where Magdalena worked were actually very understanding. At first Marco felt shy. The hotel was very fancy and cosmopolitan; it was located near the Plaza de Mayo in Buenos Aires. He immediately felt self-conscious and ashamed about his clothes and appearance. He'd never been anywhere like it. Not only was it fancy, but it was modern—all glass and gleaming, pinewood floors. He was scared to touch anything. But Magdalena's coworkers were kind, and before he knew it, he was chatting and eating a cupcake while his mother cleaned. Marco didn't want to leave when his mother told him they must hurry to get to her next job. He wished he could spend every day like this. As they held hands and ran from the hotel to a nearby office building, they smiled at each other and began to laugh. The day had gone so well.

The office building where Magdalena worked was the biggest building Marco had ever seen. It was a day of firsts. He marveled at its immensity. The elevator ride was a thrill! His mother enlisted him to empty all the wastebaskets from beneath the desks. Marco loved the job and the sense of purpose it gave him.

"Mamá! I can come every time and help you." Marco also liked the quiet, eerie feeling of the empty office, with its strangely bright lights and industrial smell, the rows of sharpened pencils and staplers, and the way he and his mother were reflected in the large glass windows. He felt suspended above Buenos Aires. Suspended above his life. As if nothing could touch them up here. They couldn't be further away from the sweat and dirt and grit of Villa Thirty-One.

It was dark by the time they finished but not that late. "I finished very fast because of you, Mijo. Let's go. There is a festival in the plaza tonight. We can walk by on our way to the bus."

"*Muy bien*, Mamá."

They took the elevator, which Marco loved, down to the lobby of the building. The doors opened to an imposing-looking man in a dark-blue suit with a bright-red tie. He looked as surprised to see them as they were to see him. Marco moved closer to his mother. He felt his mother stiffen as she cast her eyes downward in deference to this stranger.

The man glanced at a heavy gold watch on his wrist in a gesture that looked like habit. He stepped aside to make room for Magdalena and Marco to pass. Magdalena took Marco's hand, and they walked past the man. Marco wondered why it felt like they were in trouble when he knew they had done nothing wrong. The man stepped into the elevator, his well-shined shoes clicking against the floor. Just as the doors were closing, he stuck his hand out to stop them. A small chime struck to indicate the doors reopening. Marco sucked in his breath with surprise. He saw his mother bite her lip.

"*Señora*," the man said respectfully. Magdalena turned around.

"*Sí, Señor.*"

"Are you the one who cleans the twenty-second floor?"

"*Sí.*" Magdalena looked down in a way that made Marco think she was preparing herself for criticism or a reprimand.

"You do a beautiful job. It feels somehow personal. Like you care. You do your job very well, *Señora*."

"*Gracias*," Magdalena said. She squeezed Marco's hand, but she maintained a humble expression.

"Is this your son?"

"*Sí.* He normally does not come to work with me, but—" The man held up his hand to stop her.

"It's OK. I have children. I understand." The man stepped out of the stalled elevator and reached into the breast pocket of his blazer, removing a billfold made of buttery black leather. He removed several large bills. "A bonus and a thank-you." Magdalena took a step back in response. She shook her head no, saying it was not necessary. The man realized he was scaring her.

There was a table in the lobby, and the man began to walk toward it. "I will leave the money here. When I go upstairs, you take it. Please. For the child." Magdalena and Marco stared at him as he disappeared into the elevator. The lobby seemed extra quiet without his presence. Marco ran to the table and held up the money.

"Can we get ice cream at the festival now, Mamá?" Marco asked. Magdalena laughed, breaking the tension. She stuck the wad of money into the pocket of her skirt, thinking she would indulge Marco in such a rare treat.

"Of course, Mijo. Come on, let's go." It was good to see her smile. It truly had been a great day. "*Vamos por helado!*"

"Two scoops?" Marco asked, smiling a wonderfully mischievous smile. Magdalena patted her pocket with apprehension. The money and its source made her nervous. Where she came from, people didn't just hand out money, and she worried it might come with a price later. But for now, Marco was happy, and they desperately needed the money.

"Two scoops, *Mi Amor.*" As they headed to the back exit, Magdalena once again touched the pocket of her skirt. The thought crossed her mind that they should go straight home, but Marco's face was filled with such delight and anticipation that she couldn't possibly disappoint him. Besides, they deserved to have a little fun!

EIGHT

"Jose Carlo, your company is easily worth five hundred seventy-five million dollars." Jim let his words sink in for a moment. He and Jose Carlo were dining at Piegere, one of Buenos Aires's finest Italian restaurants, known as much for its pastas and risottos as its seafood and meats. The two men were seated at Jose Carlo's regular table: out of the way, but still able to see all of the action. "But you don't need the money. We both know you have more money than you could ever need," Jim said.

The two men were somewhere into their second course and already through several glasses of wine. Jose Carlo was listening attentively to Jim. The two had spent a significant amount of time together in the last forty-eight hours, and now Jim had an important question to pose. It wasn't an easy question; men like Jose Carlo often had difficulty answering it.

"Jose Carlo, let me ask you something. It might seem odd, but it's really not. In fact, I've always seen it as an essential question...What is most important to you about your money?" Jim had been afforded a good glimpse into Jose Carlo's family life, but now he needed to know where Jose Carlo stood when it came to his business. It was often a bad idea to sell companies owned by people who viewed their work as a form of self-worth. Their identities were wrapped up in their work, and they were lost when the companies sold. But an owner who learned to disconnect from the company and see the future apart from it was ready.

And if the seller was also ready, then it was really only about price. The economics were the easy part when it came to selling a family business.

There was a short silence while Jose Carlo contemplated the question. "I want to protect it. I want to be certain that I protect its value. I don't want to lose it...or do something foolish or stupid." This was a bold admission from such a powerful man.

"No one wants to be stupid, and trust me, no one wants to lose it," Jim said with a wink. "So what's really important to you about the money?" Jim asked again. There was a long silence as Jose Carlo thought. As he did, he squinted his eyes, as if trying to read something into the question.

Jim took a sip of wine. The most important thing at this moment was to let Jose Carlo work through the question. But Jim was prepared to ask a third time.

Jose Carlo laughed and shook his head. "This is not an easy question, Jim. You've got the spotlight on me." Jim assumed he meant that Jim had put him on the spot. He was about to apologize when Jose Carlo launched in. "As we discussed, my father came here with nothing. I had nothing as a child, but my father taught me to work hard.

"My cousin, Luca, and I dreamed one day of owning a home and sending our children to school. We dreamed of living near a park and taking our wives to dinner and out dancing. I never set out to build a fortune." Jose Carlo shook his head again. "This is difficult to put into words."

"Take your time," Jim said encouragingly as he listened intently.

"I want the money to be here for my family...for my father's family. This is his money and his legacy as much as it is mine. My children are responsible. They have a good work ethic, and I don't want this sort of wealth to ruin that. But I think their values are in place." Jose Carlo suddenly slapped the table. "Look, I want to see our family, my father's descendants...mine and Luca's descendants...to be in a position to build Argentina for the future. I want our grandchildren and great-grandchildren educated at the best schools. I want them to grow up and be leaders, doctors, and lawyers. But I also want them to be contributors and creators of something useful. I want them to open hospitals and libraries. The money is important to me because of what it can do for others. That's what's important to me."

"Well said," Jim said, feeling a rush of admiration for Jose Carlo. He was a blessed man. He was a good man. He was also a man who was in a state of mind to sell his business, and Jim was going to make him a lot of money.

While the men finished their meal, Jim began to crunch numbers in his head. Now that the emotional part of the transaction had been dealt with, Jim couldn't help it. It was the way his mind worked. As the dishes were cleared and coffee was served, Jim began to share his views on how the sale of Jose Carlo's company might unfold.

Before Jim had come to Buenos Aires, he had been made privy to the financial workings of Jose Carlo's company. He had been sent all of the financial statements, and things were pretty clear-cut. The business was relatively simple. It was not saddled with a lot of debt or other encumbrances. Ownership rested solely with Jose Carlo. Dinner had confirmed that there was no heir apparent to run the company; Jose Carlo's children were deeply settled in their own lives and pursuits. Jose Carlo had expressed concern for his employees and their futures, but he also believed a big, global company could benefit them.

All of this led Jim to one conclusion. As the world grew more global, the company's best path forward was to be part of a larger enterprise. Both Baker Hughes and Halliburton were likely buyers, and each needed a foothold in South America. Brazil had been first, and now the markets of Peru, Chile, and Argentina all meant more activity in South America. Companies such as Baker Hughes and Halliburton could establish a foothold on the continent with an acquisition of this kind.

As Jim continued, he could see Jose Carlo was getting tired and possibly overwhelmed. But Jim pressed on. These kinds of details needed to be hashed out in person. He counseled Jose Carlo on how to structure the sale to minimize taxes in Argentina and how much to take in cash versus stock from the acquiring company. Finally, he talked in great detail about Schlumberger and Halliburton and which would be the better fit. He knew both management teams well, but what Jim knew of Halliburton fit more closely with Jose Carlo's own priorities. Halliburton took care of its people all across the globe. It was also better positioned in some ways, and if Jim were right, by taking a portion of the sales proceeds in stock, Jose Carlo could get another 50 percent in value in the next few years as the production supercycle continued.

Just after eleven thirty, after a long dialogue and a lot of questions, Jose Carlo sighed. "Your friend did well by referring me to you, Jim. You are no-nonsense, and I have a clear sense of what lies ahead. You have created order where there was confusion and chaos." There was relief in his eyes as he smiled across the table. Jim thought Jose Carlo looked a little younger, a little softer, in this new posture of relief. Or maybe it was the late hour and the candlelight flickering over Jose Carlo's sharp features. "I feel absolutely certain of two things, Jim."

Jim nodded his head. He had a slight buzz himself at this point. "Do tell, my friend."

"First, the Segrato family will be forever grateful we were led to Jim Swanson." Jim chuckled, but he took the compliment. "Second, I am selling my company." Jose Carlo slapped the table, rattling the porcelain coffee cups and splashing coffee on the white tablecloth. Jose Carlo was not a man to show emotion or excitement, but tonight was an exception. He was elated. He'd been through a lot over the years—successes and failures, downturns and upturns, and Luca's death and the grief that followed. His father would have been proud.

"Well then," Jim said.

"Well then. I'm exhausted, I must admit, my friend," Jose Carlo said with a smile. The two men stood up from the table. "I still have things to think about, but I am confident this is the right course of action. As you have suggested, let's finalize things in the morning. I will send a car for you first thing in the morning. Give me the night to change my mind." The two men laughed, shook hands, slapped each other heartily on the back, and parted.

NINE

Jim decided to take a walk. The Four Seasons was across the street from the restaurant, but he always needed to take a walk and get some fresh air after marathon business meals like the one he had just had. He was energetic and restless by nature, which was probably the reason he was still doing triathlons at his age.

Coming out of the restaurant, he turned left and away from the Four Seasons. He walked down Calle Posadas and then turned right to stroll down Avenida 9 de Julio. Like the United States, Argentina had secured her independence through a revolution, which was celebrated on the ninth of July. This main street memorialized the country's independence. It was a grand street, with at least fifteen lanes going both ways. It rivaled New York in frenetic energy. While not as brightly lit with advertising as Times Square, it was every bit as busy. The famous street was a hallmark of the city, memorialized on postcards and in photographs as a monument to the splendor of Buenos Aires.

Jim thought about Buenos Aires's history as he walked along her crowded, charming streets with their neoclassical architecture; ornate buildings with obvious French and Italian influence and the occasional art deco beauty were popping up everywhere. The city was a major port and densely populated in the eighteen hundreds. Like the Americans, the people of Buenos Aires were frustrated with colonial rule and with the Spaniards in particular. In 1806 and 1807, Britain attempted to capture Buenos Aires to increase the empire's shipping routes. Locals valiantly defeated the attacks, giving confidence to the local people's ability to wage war.

In 1812, under the leadership of an Argentine general named Jose de San Martín, the local people fought and defeated Spain. At the Congress of Tucuman, on July 9, 1812, the country declared its independence and established the United Provinces of La Plata. In 1860, after a storied history and the eventual adoption of a constitution based largely on that of the United States, the name of the country was changed to Argentina.

San Martín would later travel over the mountains and help secure the freedom of the people of Peru and Chile as well. To this day, San Martín is revered as a national hero, like George Washington.

Jim had calculated that a brisk walk in the neighborhood would take about fifteen or twenty minutes. He planned to walk down Avenida 9 de Julio, take a left turn on Avenida Cordoba, and then another left on Avenida de Florida. Avenida de Florida was a pedestrian-only street with a shopping bazaar and mall. He would make one final left, heading straight back to the Four Seasons on Calle Posadas.

These were some of the busier parts of the city, and he considered them safe. The streets were lined with stores, busy restaurants, and hotels. As he walked, he cleared his mind and let himself drift away.

Whenever he spoke to clients about their legacies, he seemed to think about his own. He'd done well. His kids were grown and thriving. He'd given countless hours to organizations, providing leadership and helping them make important connections. He and his family had given away several million dollars to his church, schools, and other organizations.

So what was missing?

He was having an exceptional time on this trip. He was happier than he'd been in a long time. But what would happen when he went back home? More strain with Anita? This seemingly irreparable distance with his kids? He thought about his time on the vineyard and the closeness and camaraderie the Segrato family shared.

Damn. He wanted that.

And the sad truth was that he wasn't getting it. He had messed up. How had Jose Carlo managed to make a fortune and remain so close to his family? Was it all in the difference between two cultures? America was all about individualism and getting ahead on your own. Jim suddenly felt like he'd been had. He was taught to work hard. To make something of himself. To better himself. To be better and better and better.

He was not going to have what Jose Carlo had. That ship had sailed. His kids had begged him to play, come to their games, help with their homework—just hang out. And he had been too busy.

For what? For work? He was just like his own father. The only difference was that Jim had a lot of money, and his father had had little. Suddenly his whole world seemed shallow and consumeristic. What had he been thinking?

Were these unreasonable thoughts? Was he being melodramatic? He thought of Pete Matli. Pete would give anything to be Jim. Jim shook his head, trying to curb this line of thinking.

As he turned the corner onto Calle Posadas after leaving Avenida de Florida, he walked past several buildings. To his right was San Martín Park, named after the revolutionary leader General Jose de San Martín. It was late, and some sort of festival seemed to have taken place. Streamers rippled in the breeze, and vendors were packing up their wares. There was something sad about the scene.

No, that wasn't it. Yes, his life was centered on material things. That was certainly true in a sense. But just calling it consumeristic and superficial was missing the point. Disconnected. That was the problem. He and Anita were always focused in the external—giving their attention to the needs of a hospital or the opera house. These were not worthless pursuits by any stretch, but they were impersonal. He had sacrificed his relationship with his kids to be the man about town. He had sacrificed the personal.

As Jim walked on, he approached an alley on his left. When he was about five paces away from the mouth of the alley, he heard a crash and a child's yelp. He took another step and heard more noise, but this time it sounded like a woman's scream. There was a crash and a crumbling noise from the alley. These sounds seemed like those that follow a fall or an accident. Jim wondered whether something large had fallen or a collision of some sort had occurred.

Another step, and Jim was close enough to begin to see down the alley. There was more commotion and suddenly a blood-curdling scream that sent chills down Jim's back. It was a female. Something was terribly wrong. He was looking to his left, unsure of what he was hearing and trying to make sense of it, when he saw a child on the ground, clearly injured from some sort of collision. "My God, maybe something fell on the child!" he thought.

Instinctually, he turned into the alley. He needed to cover fifteen or twenty paces to reach the child. On his right, there was a Dumpster and another one past it, closer to where the child was collapsed on the ground. "Where is the woman?" he thought. Now he was walking faster and preparing to run.

Just then, the woman catapulted toward him as if she'd been thrown by an explosion. Her form, thin and slight, slammed into the wall on the other side of the alley. Before Jim could react, he saw another figure, a man's frame. Things became both confusing and clear at the same time. He had come upon some sort of mugging or attack. A boy and woman were being attacked.

The man, who had not noticed Jim, turned and bent toward the ground to grab what was probably the woman's purse or bag. His torso was now horizontal to the ground, and his head pointed toward the wall. Jim knew he had to pounce. He rushed toward the man and pushed him hard into the wall. The man was knocked to the ground. He lay there, disoriented, not knowing what had hit him.

To his left, Jim heard a runner approaching. Perceiving a threat, Jim turned to see a young wisp of a kid, no older than sixteen or seventeen, coming toward him. The kid was coming in with an attack but looked wide-eyed and scared. The kid paused, unsure what to do for a split second, but he quickly recovered and made a swipe for Jim's head. For an old man, Jim was fit, and with this fitness came speed. He ducked as the kid swung, but unfortunately the kid connected hard near Jim's ear. At fifty-four, Jim carried an older man's mass. The kid was just too light to be a genuine threat.

Adrenaline going, Jim was enraged. He quickly straightened up while the kid was completing the follow-through from the punch, and Jim popped him one. Jim's fist found the kid's eye, landing with enough impact to throw the kid's head back. The punk was off balance again. He moved his left hand to his wounded eye and moaned.

This time Jim came fully loaded. On balance and in good position, Jim's hand hit the kid perfectly in the mouth; right hand to left cheek. There was a crack and, a moment later, a crackle on the ground as the kid fell to his knees and right hand. The police would later find two teeth in the alley.

Through the corner of his right eye, Jim saw the other figure getting up. Jim saw red. He was all instinct now. His adrenaline was ramped to its peak. This other man appeared older, heavier, and far more of a threat. Rage was in charge now, but at the end of the day, Jim was a banker, and in sixty seconds things had gone from an accident to a violent crime. Fear began to creep in. Jim first pushed at the man with little effect, and then reached down to find a weapon. He picked something up and tried to swing it at the man's head in hopes of knocking him out. It was cardboard packaging or something similar—totally ineffective. Jim was in trouble.

"The older man was obviously the ringleader. And the kid was supposed to be the lookout?" Jim wondered.

"*Chingado no puedo ver!*" the older man suddenly said. What Jim didn't know was that in pushing the man into the wall, he had both disoriented him and blurred his vision. In any other situation, this man, writhing in front of Jim, would have cleaned Jim's clock. No question. He was bigger, meaner, and more desperate. But as luck would have it, Jim had an advantage. Jim's opponent was obviously scared out of his mind.

Jim looked around to find a better weapon, never really taking his eyes off of his staggering opponent. He spotted a rod about two feet long, grabbed it, and went to hit the man in the head… not too hard, but enough to neutralize the threat. The man knew enough to raise his left arm and protect himself against the hit in a swift defensive move. This time Jim reloaded, knowing the next shot would land on the arm, not the head. He came down from right to left as hard as he could against the man's arm, breaking it.

As all of this was happening, the younger of the two assailants was crawling away in defeat. With the boss losing, the kid was scared out of his wits. Little did he know that Jim was, too. There was no more rage, just fear. Jim Swanson didn't look for trouble. He'd never been mugged or held up. He was a cautious man. He was as compassionate as the next guy, but he would never have knowingly entered that alley alone if he had known a mugging was in progress.

In the moments that followed, the punk made his way from a crawl to his feet and shuffled to a run. He disappeared into the dark alley. The older thug rolled away from Jim and got to his feet, going the way of his partner. The last thing Jim remembered of either of them was the older man's side-to-side jog as he ran away, cradling his broken arm.

Jim did not move for twenty or thirty seconds. Maybe it was a minute. It felt like five. His heart was racing. "What had just happened? Wasn't he just taking a stroll only moments before? Where was he? In Argentina. In an alley..."

The child.

The child was weeping. The sound brought him to his senses. Jim quickly knelt beside the boy and assessed him. He saw no blood. The boy looked at Jim with giant, frightened eyes. Jim's heart was caught in his chest. He recovered, and from what he could tell, the boy was not injured, physically anyway. He signaled for the boy to stay put and turned to the woman.

Immediately Jim realized that she was another story. She was limp and totally unresponsive. He felt for a pulse—there was one, but it was faint. Her breathing was shallow. He could see no blood. He laid her down next to the wall. He turned to the boy and spoke.

"Niño, *tu madre es así así, pero necessito la policía. Véte a la policía! Ándale! Comprendes?*"

"Mamá," the boy whispered. His lip trembled, and his eyes were wild with fear as he approached Jim and the woman. Jim's heart went out to this boy, this stranger, as he realized this was the boy's mother. The child was in shock, but none of that mattered now. Jim needed the boy to go for help. He raised his hand and put it on the boy's shoulder softly. He began to stand up, signaling to the boy to do the same. The boy shook his head.

"*No dejo a mi mamá, no salgo.*"

Jim knelt beside the boy, putting his arm around his thin shoulders as an uncle or old friend would do. In English, Jim said, "You're OK. They are gone." He was quiet for a few seconds. "Niño. *Es importante. Policía. Comprendes tu? Para madre. Véte.*" Jim spoke in a calm voice so as to help the boy find some peace. The boy looked into Jim's eyes once again. It was obvious he was trying to see if he could trust Jim. Something occurred between them that allowed the boy to go. "*Ayúdale a mi mamá,*" the boy said. Jim nodded. "*Se llama Magdalena.*"

"*Yo comprendo,*" Jim said.

"*Ella es mi madre,* Señor." Jim felt something inside him shift. He was a father after all. He wanted to comfort the boy, but he knew the boy needed to go get help.

"*Sí,*" Jim said.

The boy broke away and ran like the wind. "*Ándale!*" Jim said, finding his voice. He turned back to the woman. Magdalena.

"Ugghh, what to do." He wasn't sure. As he thought, he felt like perhaps he should elevate her legs to help blood flow to her head and brain. Next, he laid his head across her tummy to see whether her chest was moving. She was breathing, but it was shallow. "OK, she does not need compressions or mouth-to-mouth resuscitation," he thought.

He took his blazer off and laid it over her. The temperature was comfortable but chilly, and Jim thought she might do better if she was warm. Now all he could do was monitor the situation. He used the back of his hand to stroke her cheek and forehead. He spoke softly to her in his broken Spanish and English. He told her that her son was safe and needed her. "Stay with me," he said softly.

Soon the boy returned with an officer. Sirens began to fill the air. The officer spoke no English. He asked Jim some questions but soon realized that they were not going to be able to communicate well enough.

It took about ten minutes for the woman and the child to be evacuated. Jim watched as their ambulance tore away into the night. Jim was put in the back of another ambulance for evaluation. He was given water and a cold pack for his head and right knuckles, but he felt OK. The medical team found no reason to take him to a hospital.

The cop who didn't speak English was smart and had thought to ask his supervisor to send someone who spoke English. Jim might be someone important. He was certainly dressed well.

Jim had to sit in the ambulance for about twenty-five more minutes until a detective arrived. This man appeared to be very senior and spoke impeccable English. Jim recapped what he could recall and answered every question as well as he could. He and the boy's story matched, so there were no concerns from the detective's perspective.

The detective deposited Jim at his hotel. It was about one thirty in the morning when Jim finally fell into bed. His dinner with Jose Carlo seemed a world away. He thought about calling Anita, but he was too exhausted from the trauma of the night. He was too tired to think straight. All he could do was sleep. He'd think in the morning.

TEN

It was nine o'clock when Jim's Blackberry rang.

Jim shot up in response. He had been in a deep sleep, and the phone had startled him. He panicked, in part because he could tell it was late by the amount of light coming into the room. Jim usually rose early, and his waking moments were often in darkness illuminated by the dim glow of an alarm clock. His hotel room was lit up with sunlight. Jim panicked for a moment. What time was it? He was so used to waking up in the dark. Had he missed his meeting with Jose Carlo? Suddenly the events of the previous night flashed through his head.

"Was that real?"

He answered the phone.

"Señor Swanson?" The voice on the other end of the line was no-nonsense and carried a heavy accent.

"Yes, this is he."

"This is Detective Santorini with the Buenos Aires Police Department."

"Oh," Jim rubbed his eyes. Last night had been real.

"Señor, you asked me to call you as soon as I had news of the woman."

"Of course. Please," Jim said.

"I regret to inform you, but she has died."

Jim gasped, bringing his hand to his mouth. "Jesus."

"She was severely injured in the attack because of a blow to her head." The detective waited for Jim to respond. When Jim didn't say anything, he continued. "You were very brave to have helped her." There was a pause as the detective searched for the right words. "I am sorry."

"Oh, God." Jim took a deep, heavy breath. How tragic. How senseless. There was a long silence. Jim uttered a silent prayer. "Please, God, give her peace and bring her home."

"Señor?"

"Yes, I am here. Detective, I am very sorry to hear this news. What do you know about the boy?" Jim's mind was becoming more fully alert as he began to replay last night's events.

"He has not been told, and he will stay in the hospital today. The social services people are going to speak to him this morning, but we have not identified any family or relatives. I think they are peasants. I have a hunch they live in Villa Thirty-One." Jim didn't say anything in response. He was processing what the detective was saying. "Do you know this place?"

"No," Jim said definitively. He was stuck on the idea of this kid being told by a social worker that his mother had just died.

"No, why would you? It is a poor place where the conditions are, well, miserable. If he was a resident of Villa Thirty-One, he will probably be taken to an orphanage. The people there are poor, and often kids live in fatherless homes. It is very tragic, but this move will be good for the boy...Our orphanages need improvement, but they are better than growing up in a shantytown."

"An orphanage?" Jim said, shaking his head.

"Villa Thirty-One is not a place for children, if you know what I mean."

"Thank you for following up with me, Detective." This man was not completely insensitive, but he was obviously jaded, and Jim didn't want to talk to him anymore. After he hung up the phone, he found he was fully awake and alert.

The first thing Jim did was to call Jose Carlo on his private cell phone.

"*Bueno*," Jose Carlo said.

"Jose Carlo, I am going to be late this morning, and I might need your help."

Jim shared the previous night's events in as much detail as he could. Jose Carlo was engaged and attentive. He was both captivated and concerned. He asked a few questions to ascertain whether Jim himself needed medical attention.

Jim asked Jose Carlo if he could help him find the hospital and the boy. He explained that he wanted to see what he could do to help the child. Jose Carlo would call his son Roberto, the cardiologist. Roberto could work around the system and perhaps find out some information.

After their discussion, Jose Carlo informed Jim that his driver Hector would be by to collect him soon.

Later in the morning, Jose Carlo's son was able to get some details by poking around and asking questions. The boy was still at the hospital, waiting for family members to be located. He had learned of his mother's fate from a busy, overworked social services advocate who had arrived several hours after his mother's death. As she sat with Marco, she glanced often at her watch. She needed to be off soon to make at least two more visits before punching out. Taking a page from her training, she wanted to be clear and direct. "I am sorry, but after your mamá arrived at the hospital, the team of doctors and nurses fought valiantly to give her every chance. She was strong, but the injuries were just too great; she did not survive the trauma. With head injuries, survival often comes with so many hindrances that it may have actually been for the better. Don't worry; you'll be fine. We'll have your family here any minute. I am sure your father is coming. When he gets here, give him my card, and we can arrange for further assistance. Again, I am sorry to deliver this news." It never occurred to her that speaking to a ten-year-old was different from speaking with an adult.

Crime brings both grief and loss. This kid was just another lost soul in a big city. He would likely find his way to an orphanage. "Too bad" was the general consensus—most people were relatively unconcerned.

Jim next called Coco at his office to prepare for the meetings regarding the sale of Jose Carlo's company, which were to resume later that morning. Because of Jim's late start, the meeting was pushed back to ten o'clock. Jim spoke to one of his partners and to a few VPs in Houston who were reviewing merger docs provided by Klyner Peabody. He told the team to focus on Halliburton as the acquirer. He also debriefed the team on the salient elements that Jose Carlo was looking for, as well as the deal structure they had outlined the night before.

He instructed the team on several action items, including calling their friends at Andrews Kurth, a law firm that specialized in M&A activity, and PwC, the global accounting firm. He wanted the best teams to review Jose Carlo's tax implications with the structure they were contemplating. Often subtle elements and structural changes could significantly influence the net after-tax impact of a transaction. He wanted to have the best outcome for the Segrato family.

He also had them arrange a midday conference call with Klyner Peabody's senior partner working on the transaction. This would give Jim time to brief Jose Carlo, work through some details, and reconfirm key points. They would discuss in greater detail conditions around timing from Jose Carlo's perspective. Another important element Jim always focused on was how the owner went public with the information. Some families wanted to bring those closest to them up to speed before an announcement became public, while others preferred to address the transaction after the news hit.

ELEVEN

Father Diaz had stabilized everything for Marco. The day following the incident was confusing and complicated for him. At first he was unsure of his mother's status. The adults had spoken to him and asked him several times whether he understood. Trying to be agreeable, he'd nodded his head. But the social worker's haste to end her day, and her perception that a direct and candid conversation would be best in this situation, did little to help Marco understand. In reality, he had not followed any of the adults at the hospital and had spent that entire day asking when he could see his mother.

It wasn't until late that evening when Father Diaz arrived at the hospital that he first saw someone he knew. First the priest greeted Marco, and then he disappeared for a long time. Marco did not know at that point that Father Diaz was helping with final arrangements for Magdalena's body. Father Diaz had been down this path before, but never with someone who'd been close to him. He'd come to know Magdalena and Marco well. There was never a hint of impropriety, but for a man who'd vowed himself to celibacy, some of their time on Saturdays had felt a bit like having a family, with a woman to care for his needs and a son to tutor. Since Marco was so often the only student, even though other members of the parish had been invited, they'd become especially close.

Father Diaz finally appeared again, this time with a long face. It was then that Marco could sense dread. It was Father Diaz who slowed the conversation down enough, asking the right questions and explaining things in the right way, that Marco could fully comprehend that his mother was dead. It was his first time to fully encounter death, something surprising given the crime in Villa Thirty-One, but also a testament to the shelter his mother had provided as protection for the boy.

After the crime, with Father Diaz's help, the police had found Rosa, Marco's aunt, living in Villa Thirty-One. As had been anticipated, the boy's opportunity there was dim. Throughout the investigation, Jim had maintained frequent contact with the detective. He'd also mentioned that he was going to try and provide some funds for the boy's care. The detective was careful not to mention Jim or his financial support before he had assessed Rosa's character. It was not inconceivable that she would try to work out a deal where she'd be paid for Marco's care, but would in reality neglect the boy. It was apparent that she desperately needed the money. Her sister's contribution to the family's needs had made the days and weeks a little easier. With her out of the picture, Rosa was in an even greater state of poverty. To give her the benefit of the doubt, it seemed she thought Marco would be better off in an orphanage.

Marco didn't want to be with Rosa, either, which seemed to settle the question.

In traveling back and forth to Argentina the following weeks concluding the sale of Jose Carlo's company, Jim extended one of his stays to help establish plans for Marco. With the detective's help, Jim was able to connect with Father Diaz and asked for a meeting. The priest thought it would be best for the boy to see Jim. The detective had permitted Marco's release to the priest while Jim was working out what he might be able to do to provide support for the boy.

During this first meeting, Marco sat outside the office. It was a small church, which had a small office. Jim thought, as he sat down across from the priest, that his own walk-in closet dwarfed this man's work space. There was a tall bookcase along one wall, a small window up high on another, and the man's desk against a third wall. Atop the desk was an ancient computer. It looked like a handmade computer from some years ago, and Jim could tell both the computer and the monitor were turned off.

Marco sat quietly near the desk of one of the parish nuns and had been sitting outside for what seemed like an eternity. There was no indication he'd done anything wrong, but as time elapsed, he began to worry.

From outside, Marco could hear some talking. It was difficult to make out the sounds, but he was certain they were speaking in a hushed tone. He also suspected they were speaking in a foreign language.

Father Diaz knew Marco was smart and would benefit from an education, and he told Jim as much. He agreed to ensure that the boy's daily needs and home environment would be met until high school. The boy would stay with the parish, under the care of the priest, the parish nuns, and their congregation, but he would be financially underwritten by Jim through a trust. The bishop appreciated that the generous stipend would have an impact on the poor church and help the diocese subsidize the parish.

Within a month following the death of Magdalena, Father Diaz and Jim organized most of the key elements, and Marco had a path outside of the orphanage. After Jim's first meeting, Father Diaz began to explain to the boy what the man from America was doing.

"Marco. Senior Swanson is very fond of you and wants to help you go to a good school and continue your studies. He will help us take care of you here at the church. And as you get older, he will help you attend a high school where you can continue your studies. You are very blessed, Marco." Father Diaz said.

Still grieving and confused, Marco offered little in response, hoping to be obedient and respectful of Father Diaz. The priest was Marco's only sense of family left.

Anita was dismissive and indifferent. Her questions about Jim's new "project" were focused on the social impact, or better yet, how she could brag about it to her friends. She also expected that in time, after a few checks were written, Jim's passion would fade.

Jim left no stone unturned. He was laser focused, excited, and completely committed to his plan. He felt for the first time in his life he was really doing something meaningful and genuinely selfless. It was exhilarating! While it was some time off, Jim had even connected through his own alma mater to a Jesuit boarding school in Argentina for boys beginning at age fourteen. This would provide Marco a chance to get a good education and maybe make something more out of his life. All Jim needed now was one final piece of the plan.

TWELVE

"Jose Carlo, I need a favor," Jim said, sitting in his office in Houston. He had his legs up on his desk and was looking out his window from the seventy-third floor of the Chase Tower. He looked east toward the Houston Ship Channel and the city's industrial complex. Most people preferred the west view, where they could see the skyline of Houston's Galleria and a topography punctuated by live oak trees and the winding roads of Allen Parkway and Memorial Drive that carried many home to their affluent and comfortable suburbs. But Jim preferred to look east, where industry punctuated all one could see. Looking this direction, just past Minute Maid Park, home of the Houston Astros, Jim observed Houston's East Side and Second Ward, a poor urban enclave that was seeing modest redevelopment. But beyond this, he could see the flames of gas flares from refineries and a sunlit shining glimmer from Trinity Bay beyond. The bay fed the Houston Ship Channel through to Galveston Bay and the Gulf of Mexico. Jim liked the east view because it gave him a view of Houston's commercial district, where thriving businesses intersected with industry to create fortunes.

"What can I do for you?" Jose Carlo was intrigued, but at the same time caught a little off guard. He too sat in his own office, in Argentina. The men just ended a conference call in which deal

81

terms were reviewed, closing considerations were ironed out, and dates were set. In the previous eight weeks, Jim and Jose Carlo had been working closely together on the sale of Jose Carlo's business. Jim had visited Argentina almost weekly, and during his many trips, he'd included time to work out a plan to help the orphaned boy, Marco. But Jim was going to need help. He could only do so much from Houston.

Jose Carlo was elated with the work done by Jim and his firm. Jose Carlo was about to make $600 million dollars and transition to new endeavors of his own.

"I've made a decision to help provide for the boy," Jim said.

"The boy?" Jose Carlo was momentarily lost, but in a moment, he realized whom Jim was referring to. As the thought connected, Jim reminded him.

"The orphan boy; his name is Marco. I have decided to help him and have put some things in place. But I have some problems with what I am trying to do, and I need your help. Will you give me a few minutes and let me map out what I am trying to do?"

"Absolutely. Tell me, my friend."

"I connected with a close friend of Marco's family, a Father Manuel Diaz. The boy's mother used to work for him at his parish, cleaning the church and helping with parish activities. The police found an aunt living in Villa Thirty-One after Father Diaz directed them there. Marco does not want to live with her, and the aunt said she was unwilling to take responsibility for him. She herself is poor and has her own children. Her sister's contribution to the family's needs made the days and weeks a little easier. But with Magdalena out of the picture, the aunt is in an even greater state of poverty.

"Apparently, the boy and the priest are very close, and in fact, in speaking with Father Diaz, it seems as if he has become a father figure to Marco. Marco's welfare is genuinely of great concern for the priest. In fact, the boy has been staying with the priest at the church since his mother's death. Father Diaz has offered to continue to provide shelter for the boy, and his bishop has agreed to allow me to provide funds for the boy's living and educational needs. He would remain in the church community and the priest would be responsible for him. If I—"

"Mr. Swanson," Jose Carlo said. The last time he'd called Jim "Mr. Swanson" was at the *estancia* on Jim's first visit. "I believe what you desire to do is noble. It reflects well on your character, and you know my family and I are grateful for your efforts. You indeed are a very honorable and devoted man. But we cannot be involved in raising the boy. I am old, and Cecilia and I are far from interested in having a—"

"No, no!" This time it was Jim's turn to interrupt, as he was laughing with a big smile on his face. "Jose Carlo, I need something very simple, really. Please, let me explain. I believe in order for me to provide funds for the boy from the United States, it will be necessary to do so through a conduit such as a trust. All I am really asking is whether, as an Argentine natural citizen, you will serve, or ask your lawyer to serve, as an administrator and trustee. I will fund the trust and instruct disbursements to Father Diaz or the boy's school as needed. Essentially, all I am seeking is someone to make the payments upon my request."

"I do not need to meet the boy or meet with the priest?"

"No," Jim said.

"I will not be involved with this Father Diaz, have any legal obligations, need to rescue some drug addict, or have to bail any juvenile out of jail?"

"No."

"All I have to do is provide administration of the trust you are establishing and have someone on my staff make payments to Diaz...or I guess to whomever you tell us to make payments?"

"Yes! Exactly," Jim said.

"Jim, you have done us a great service. I am not sure this is a boy worth your investment. In fact, I fear you are making a mistake and wasting your money. The boy is from the ghetto. But if it is important to you, I will do it. We will be happy to do this for you."

A few days later, Jose Carlo Segrato was in his boardroom with a number of his closest staff members. He'd handpicked four individuals from his company to join his family office, including his general counsel and a young finance professional who worked on special projects for his CFO. They were wrapping up a series of loose ends on gifts Jose Carlo was making as part of a comprehensive estate plan, and they had come to the final item on the day's agenda.

The general counsel was leading the discussion. "Señor, we have everything in place for the boy's trust. I've worked with Mr. Swanson to ensure the language is consistent with his expectations, and his local attorneys have given us the green light to execute the trusts. As you requested, you have no obligation whatsoever. You will serve as the trustee for the trust and make disbursements as needed and when requested by Mr. Swanson. All we need to do is add the boy's name and have you execute the documents by signing where indicated."

"Let's do this. Where do I sign?" Jose Carlo asked.

"Please sign these three documents, which are part of the trust, and then I'll add the boy's name on pages one and seven, the only two places he is referenced."

Jose Carlo started signing as they handed the documents over. "I am now leaving for Mendoza. Let's pick this up when I return next week."

"Señor Segrato, I need the boy's name. I know it is Marco, but I need his family name."

"What did Jim say his name was?" Jose Carlo asked.

"That's kind of the problem. He could not recall the boy's last name."

"I don't want a lot of trouble with this." Jose Carlo was thinking of the easiest way to move this forward and expected Swanson's support wouldn't last that long. "Can we just name the boy Marco Segrato? I mean, let's just name the boy Marco Segrato to make it easier on us, and we can ensure no one ever shows up asking for money. What do you think?"

The lawyer shrugged his shoulder. He liked the idea and agreed as he thought that someone could show up one day laying claim to money intended for the boy. "Yes, let's do that."

BOOK TWO
SUMMER'S WINTER

THIRTEEN

"Marco!"

"What?" Marco's eyes were closed, but his full lips were curved into a smile.

"Slow down, cowboy!" Marco opened his eyes. Lily was staring down at him. She looked beautiful. It was Friday, and instead of wearing her school uniform, she had on a Rolling Stones T-shirt and jeans. She looked perfect.

"Sorry. You're just so cute!" Marco said sincerely. He playfully wrestled Lily onto her back and kissed her forehead. They were laughing one moment, but in the next, Lily was staring at Marco with her big, brown eyes set in her cherubic round face. "She's part angel," Marco thought to himself. But something in her look frightened him. There was a certainty there that he himself didn't feel. He looked back at her and forced a smile. "We better get going. My roommate will be back soon."

A quick look of hurt flashed over Lily's face, but she quickly sat up and straightened her shirt and hair. Marco felt bad. Lily was his best friend. She was more, but he didn't know exactly what. He was seventeen years old, terrifically good looking, smart, and athletic, but he was painfully shy with girls. Most girls. But Lily was just a friend. He tried to convince himself.

At seventeen, Marco was more boy than man. Life had thrown him some tough times, and he carried with him a certain melancholy. He was burdened with a hard sense of responsibility for someone so young. But in the end, he was *still* a seventeen-year-old boy with seventeen-year-old hormones. He just wasn't ready to be someone's boyfriend. But Lily wasn't just someone, and he shouldn't be fooling around with her like this if he didn't want to be her boyfriend.

"It's OK, Marco, you're leaving tomorrow. It's cool." Marco took Lily's hand. He knew she was putting on a brave face. Tomorrow morning he would leave to spend summer break in Houston, but Lily would be stuck at school. And if it weren't for Jim Swanson, Marco would be, too. Both kids were scholarship students at Colegio del Salvador, the Jesuit boarding school they had both attended since they were fourteen.

Marco's iPhone suddenly vibrated on the small bedside table next to his twin bed. Jim's name flashed on the screen, accompanied by a flattering photo of his "uncle" finishing one of his triathlons.

"His ears must be burning," Lily said. She stood up and went to get her backpack off Marco's desk. There wasn't much room for privacy in the tiny dorm room, but Marco appreciated her effort. Jim was calling to discuss the final travel plans for Marco's flight the next morning. It was a short, friendly conversation. Marco was excited to see Jim and excited to see his Houston friends. He got off the phone and took Lily into his arms.

"I'm not going to cry," she said.

"I'll call you all the time and text every hour on the hour," Marco said, smiling.

"You don't have to do that. But you do have to get me out of here before we get caught."

"That I can do!" He grabbed her hand, and they began their stealthy exit from the boys' wing.

FOURTEEN

"Ladies and Gentlemen, the captain has indicated our final approach into Houston Bush Intercontinental Airport. Please put your tray tables away in the locked position and bring your seat backs forward for landing."

Marco shook himself awake. Had he slept through the whole flight? The flight attendant continued to speak. "At this time, a member of the service crew will be coming through the cabin to collect any remaining trash or other items you would like to dispose of. On behalf of United Airlines, we want to thank you for your business and this opportunity to serve you. If Houston is your final destination with us, please enjoy your stay." The familiar chime sounded as the modern airliner slowly descended into the airport. Marco had made this flight every year since he was eleven years old.

These trips were always fun. He enjoyed seeing the Swansons. And to be honest, it gave him a chance to see how the other half lived. Most of his peers at Colegio del Salvador were extremely wealthy. Even though Marco had spending money, thanks to the Swansons, the divide between him and the other students was apparent. Like Lily, Marco never left the school on the weekends because there was nowhere for him to go. Most of his friends left every Friday night. Sure, he joined them sometimes, but he always felt like an outsider, and no one knew where he was really from. Villa Thirty-One was a deeply buried secret, as if this part of his history had been erased. It was just too painful to go anywhere near those memories. Lily had an idea, but even she, as close as they were, didn't know the details. Marco was still very much in touch with Father Diaz, and when Marco needed to dip down into that dark place that was his childhood, he would go for a visit and a talk. Father Diaz and the parish were like family to Marco—a family of sorts.

While Marco didn't enjoy any extravagances, thanks to the Swansons, his basic needs were met and then some. In fact, the Swanson family had been incredibly generous. Every summer for the last six years, Marco had gotten a reprieve from being the scholarship kid. These reprieves came in the form of a summer trip to stay with Jim and Anita in Houston, Texas.

While Marco's friends in Argentina would vacation with their own families, get together for shopping and movie dates, hit the beaches, or visit their estancias in Mendoza or Patagonia for extended periods, Marco would go to Houston. As Marco waited for his luggage to come down the conveyor belt, he let himself wonder what it might be like to date a girl from Houston this summer. As with all boys his age, his mind seemed to race between sports, girls, jesting with his buddies, and girls. His thoughts drifted to a few girls he'd met over the years; each year his English improved, and he seemed more likely to make a connection. He looked across the conveyor belt, noticed three girls about his age, and smiled at one. She smiled back, stroking his confidence.

His thoughts were interrupted by the ringing bell and blinking light indicating the conveyor belt was about to begin passing luggage from his flight. The bell startled him, and for a moment, he remembered Lily with a sense of guilt for thinking of other girls. He brushed the thought of her aside. She wasn't his girlfriend. He had made that clear. He loved her, but he wasn't sure he loved her in *that* way. In fact, Marco wasn't really sure what love was. In his visits with Father Diaz, they often seemed to return to love. Father Diaz would talk about how much God loved them and how God's love was perfect, but each of them knew that having lost his mother, Marco had lost a type of love that is without comparison. It was one of the reasons he guarded his history so closely, and yet he longed, deep in his heart, to find a girlfriend with whom he could share these memories and satisfy his longing to be close, really close, to someone.

He had met girls at some of the school's dances and made out a little here and there (mostly here and there with Lily), but he was definitely a virgin. He also kept that secret hidden from his friends—a nice group of guys, but they would rib him to death if they knew the truth. Truth was, half of them were probably virgins, too. Marco laughed to himself at the thought.

"Dude! You're becoming a giant!" Marco's reverie was interrupted as a hand landed softly on his shoulder. It was Jim Swanson.

Marco turned and greeted the man. They spoke English. Marco could switch from Spanish to English without thinking these days. He had a heavy accent, but as far as Jim was concerned, that was part of Marco's long list of charms.

"Hey, Jim!" Marco said. It felt good to see Jim. A coming home of sorts.

"How was the flight?"

"Tiring of course." Marco smiled. "And I don't fit well in the seats...I'd rather be in first class," Marco said, hinting, and then laughed.

"Get a good job, and you can fly first class on your own nickel. Change the world, and you can charter your own plane!"

"Ha, ha."

"I'm serious," Jim said.

"Yeah! I know you are!"

Jim slapped Marco on the back, and the two laughed as they exited the airport. "Anita is throwing a small dinner party to welcome you home," Jim said as he threw Marco's bags into the trunk.

"Oh," Marco said, surprised. The thought of a dinner party in his honor made him more than a little uncomfortable, and Anita didn't do anything small. Jim seemed to read his mind.

"Just the kids! I swear. Just the kids." Marco let out a sigh of relief. "She's got her hands full with Thanksgiving a week away," Jim said. Marco nodded with understanding. Planning one of her famous Thanksgivings would keep Anita busy for sure.

Marco watched Jim as he steered his large Mercedes out of the airport, telling stories about his races and his work with animation and excitement. Jim had really changed over the years. It had been sort of subtle as it was happening, but now Marco could see the change was undeniable. Jim was happier. Softer. He listened differently when Marco spoke. He had always been kind, tremendously kind, but distracted. Now Jim seemed totally present, with a megawatt grin and all sorts of crazy energy. Jim must have felt Marco studying him.

"What is it? Do I have something on my face?" Jim said, half joking.

"No, no." Marco said. He felt funny saying this, but decided to anyway. "You just seem happy, Jim."

Jim was silent for a moment. Marco's comment had taken him off guard. Then he began to nod his head. "I am. I am. Things aren't perfect," he said quietly. Marco assumed Jim was talking about Anita—they seemed to have a complicated marriage—but that was none of Marco's business. "But things are good." Jim kept nodding. "Things are good."

FIFTEEN

"Marco!" Anita screamed as Jim and Marco came through the garage and into the Swansons' impressive kitchen. Jim watched as she ran to the boy, threw her small arms around his enormous frame, and rattled off her greeting in Spanish. Jim felt a small spike of envy. The days when she had greeted him like that were long gone. Probably gone forever. Jim shook it off. The state of his marriage was what it was, and they had both grown fairly comfortable with that. He wasn't going to let it drag him down. Not today anyway. Marco was home!

Jim and Anita had quickly accepted Marco into their family after the tragic event of his mother's brutal death. They treated him not quite like a son, but more like a nephew who often came to visit. They provided for him as if he were the son of one of their siblings who had lost his parents. Pretty much anything Marco ever needed was provided, usually through Father Diaz or through the dean of students at the Colegio del Salvador. Jim saw to that.

Marco had spent Thanksgiving and Christmas with the Swansons and their family for the last six years, while it was summer in the Southern Hemisphere and his high school was on break. All the Swanson children were grown. Jim and Anita's grandchildren were young, so within their family, he was between the generations. When he was there with Jim and Anita, he was like a surprise baby conceived late in life, but better. They hadn't had to raise an infant or a toddler. By the time the incident that brought them together occurred, he was over ten years old, capable of taking care of himself and being tutored and chauffeured by a nanny.

Each summer, the Swansons hired a Rice University student, usually a girl, to work with Marco on English and help him on summer lessons, using some resources from the Keystone School, which provided accredited homeschooling curriculum for many different states. Anita Swanson would communicate in the early fall with Colegio del Salvador to review what course work Marco would have in the coming year, and with these tools and a reliable college student, they'd organize a pretty extensive homeschool day for Marco. The boy lightly bristled at this, saying it was his summer break, but he always came around.

This year, Jim had something different in mind for Marco. He wanted him to work part-time at his office.

In addition to his studies, Marco would play basketball through the Swansons' church league. He was, as expected, an outstanding soccer player. He was now on the varsity team at Salvador and was one of its captains. From what Jim gathered, the coaches liked Marco's grit and his fight. You never wanted to be on an opposing team if there was a game brawl. Marco was rough when mad and could take a licking. To hear Marco tell it, he won fights both because he could hit hard and because he never backed down, no matter how hard he was hit. This was not to say he got in fights often or was a troublemaker. He was a good kid. But when someone he cared about was picked on, or if the rich kids came at him because of his history, he'd fight back with all of his might. Jim knew this from reports from the principal of Marco's school. It was apparent that Marco hated the strong picking on the weak. You never wanted to be a bully around Marco Segrato. If you did, the devil in him was unleashed. And Jim couldn't blame him. After what he'd been through, Marco would probably spend his whole life trying to right that wrong.

Marco would also complete his Eagle Scout project this year. Jim was very excited about this. Since Marco's first visit, he'd been involved in scouting with Jim. Jim's own sons were Eagle Scouts, and as a "Gray Hair," Jim enjoyed this time in the scouting program. Having Marco in town always gave Jim a greater excuse to stay involved. Scouting also helped equip Marco for life, as it had Jim's own sons over a decade earlier. They were active in a large troop in the center of town. It was comprised of boys from many private schools, including the most elite schools in Houston. For Marco, these friends were of the same cut as those back in Argentina, but it was different. Here in America, Marco might as well have been one of them. He'd ride to events and activities in Jim's Mercedes. If friends came over to play video games or hang out, especially when Christmas break began, the Swansons' house was similar to theirs.

"Whoa. Do you see that, Anita?" Jim heard Marco say, interrupting his thoughts.

"I do, Marco. I can see the gears just grinding away in that big brain," Anita said playfully. More playfully than Jim had probably heard her sound since the last time Marco had been there, if he thought about it. "Let's give the boy a meal before you unleash your winter agenda on him. What do you say, Jim?" Anita said.

Jim laughed in response. "Fair enough." He found himself blushing a little. The romance might have left his marriage, but Anita knew him better than anyone. For that he would always love her.

Anita left the guys with a plate of sandwiches that would feed ten men and a spread of potato chips, soda, and a pie for dessert while she set off for a match at the club. She didn't even ask Jim to join her anymore, and that was fine with him. He tried to avoid the club at all costs these days. He even worked out at a different gym closer to his office. The club was just too political, and Jim didn't have the stomach for it anymore. He had met workout buddies through his races that he found more, well, more down-to-earth. Jim watched as Marco tore into the bountiful spread with glee, and he chuckled. Sometimes teenage boys were so easy to please.

Jim's thoughts drifted back to Anita as he ate his own sandwich. He and Anita had been married a long time. Like many marriages, theirs had survived some rough patches. They were faithful and religious, but they had survived by allowing each other to go different ways at times. Anita was a reputable interior decorator. She had a high-end clientele, some of whom were also Jim's clients, and these days she was known to spend a month on location at a client's new home somewhere like Colorado, Santa Fe, or Sanibel Island. They both participated in Marco's visits, but the nanny was primarily responsible for his activities. Anita would organize the schooling and the tutoring, and Jim would organize the basketball, the scouting, and the skiing. It was great for both of them because after a few months, Marco went back home. The empty nest got a little activity for a short period of time, and then Jim and Anita could drift off to their own interests of work and travel.

Anita, Jim, and Marco fell into the normal routine for the coming weeks and through Thanksgiving and Christmas. Jim spent a lot of evenings with Marco. Anita spent mornings with him, and Maria, their longtime housekeeper, spent the days with him when he wasn't involved in some studies or curriculum with the Rice nanny. And maybe a few days a week this time, Jim hoped Marco would come to the office with him and earn a little money.

Jim and Anita hadn't discussed it, but looking at Marco now, the years of finding some college girl to tutor Marco were probably coming to an end. He was all man now: handsome, dark, smart, and available. Sure, they were older, but it hadn't escaped Jim and Anita that last year, toward the end of his time in the States, something had been heating up between Marco and his tutor. Nothing had happened, at least Jim didn't think it had, but if things had gone on much longer, the two had been destined for romance.

"So, Kiddo. This trip is going to be a little different," Jim said, as Marco finished a slug of his Sprite. Marco listened in silence, waiting for what was to come. "You're going to come to work with me."

"Work with you?" Marco said politely. This was where Marco differed from Jim's own children. That sentence would have set off whines and complaints instantly. Marco may have felt the same sentiment, but there was still a politeness between them that had never fully gone away.

Jim almost wished Marco felt the deep comfort that would have made him act just a bit spoiled or entitled. Jim brushed the thought away. "Yes, work. It's time to learn a little bit about the business world and make some money."

"I'll get paid?" Marco's eyes lit up.

"Yes. Not enough to fly home first class, Buddy, but yes, you'll get paid," Jim said.

"Cool," Marco said, dipping his hand into a bag of potato chips. "Cool. I gotta go take a leak." Jim laughed. Marco really had learned to speak English well.

SIXTEEN

There wasn't one person at the table who wasn't thankful when the doorbell rang. JJ, Mary, and Sarah, Jim's adult children, had come with their spouses and children to celebrate Marco's arrival. Anita had cooked a beautiful dinner—two large roast chickens, saffron rice, and several gorgeous vegetable platters. The food had been gobbled up quickly, as Jane, Mary, and Sarah ran after their toddlers and young children most of the dinner, and the moms weren't very happy about it. Something had occurred between Anita and her daughters just after they arrived, but Marco didn't know what it was. All four women seemed withdrawn and irritated. He hoped it had nothing to do with his arrival. He had always wondered whether his presence annoyed the Swanson kids. He could see how it would.

JJ was his affable self, but he wasn't lifting a finger to help Jane, and Marco could see why she was angry. Mary and Sarah's husbands were taking a play from JJ's book. Jim was actually chasing after his grandchildren, which Marco had never seen before. "Good for him," he thought.

Everyone had been wrangled back to the table for dessert, but there had been a thick, uncomfortable silence until the doorbell suddenly rang.

Maria answered the door to the whoops and hollers of Marco's Houston crew. They rolled into the Swansons' foyer like a litter of puppies. Marco was thrilled to see them and totally thankful for the distraction from Anita's failed dinner party. A lot of high-fives and back-slapping hugs ensued. Marco, usually more reserved, couldn't help but share in the boys' infectious excitement. Two stunningly beautiful teenage girls stood aside, quietly watching the scene.

Chris, the leader of the pack, turned his baseball hat backward and took a long look at Marco. "Damn, dude! You grew! You're huge!"

Marco had met Chris on his first visit to the States, while playing in the church's basketball league. But the bonds were tied when, in the subsequent week, they had attended a campout for scouts. Between the two activities, the boys were always having fun. While Marco's English was tolerable that holiday season, Chris, who'd studied Spanish since he was two, had helped Marco begin to develop his language skills. Marco knew the other guys from the scouting program as well.

"Just what I told him at the airport," Jim said from the dining room table.

"Ahem, hello, Chris?" one of the girls said.

"Oh my gosh, Abigail, Emily, I am so sorry, Dudes."

"Chris, don't call the girls 'dudes,'" Anita said.

"Sorry, Mrs. Swanson." Chris turned red. Anita was still enough of a beauty to make a sixteen-year-old punk like Chris blush.

Introductions were made, and the Swanson kids and their young children—the grandchildren—took the opportunity to make their adieus for the night. Marco noticed Jim watching with pride as his own children expertly packed diaper bags and strollers and tenderly carried their children out of the Swansons' mansion.

Once again, Marco noted how much Jim had changed over the years. Marco was still forming the words for it. Tender? Maybe, but really it was that there was so much more there. Jim wasn't pulled in fifty different directions the way he used to be when Marco had first started coming for these visits. Jim would have never helped his daughters out the way he had tonight. He was now totally into them and his grandkids. It was awesome. That's the kind of dad Marco wanted to be one day. He would never be too busy for his kids—never.

"Marco, I've heard so much about you." The blond girl, Abigail, suddenly approached Marco with an outstretched hand. She wore a white cashmere sweater and jeans tucked into boots. She was petite and sort of intimidatingly perfect. Her small nails were painted with white tips, and she wore a gold necklace that spelled out the word "Abigail" on a thin gold chain around her neck. Small diamond studs glittered from her ears. Her hair was blown out, and her eyes were lined in black; her lips were shiny with pale-beige lipstick and gloss.

"Nice to meet you," Marco said shyly. It was obvious Abigail was a girl who knew the power of her beauty. There were girls like this at his school in Buenos Aires, but Marco had never had the nerve to talk to them. He thought of Lily. This girl was the opposite of Lily.

"Do you need any help with these dishes?" Abigail asked Anita. Marco felt the twang of her accent in his kneecaps. He was in trouble.

"You're such a kiss ass, Ab," Chris said.

"Language, Chris!" Jim said.

Emily, who had been mostly silent up to that point, piped up. "I think we are going to miss the movie if we don't get going."

"What would we do without our secretary?" Josh, one of the other boys, asked. Marco and Jim had known these guys for years. They were Eagle Scouts together. Marco noticed Emily's pale cheeks blush pink at Josh's tease. Marco studied Emily for a moment.

She was pretty in a quiet way—a way that he could relate to. She had long red hair that was braided down her back. Her skin was fair and dotted with charming freckles. Her energy was more like Lily's—smart, quiet. It took up much less space than Abigail's highly polished superwattage. Just as Marco was thinking this, Abigail seemed to sense Marco's attention was off her for a moment and stepped in. She put her arm through Marco's, which made him shudder slightly as she was so magnetic. He desperately hoped she hadn't noticed.

"You're right, Em. As always," Abigail said sincerely. Marco noticed how Abigail seemed to take the attention off Emily and throw her a compliment in one fell swoop. He smiled shyly at Emily as if to say sorry, but for what he didn't know. For having a prettier, more charismatic friend? He saw this dynamic all the time at school—a beauty and her faithful sidekick. Marco was sure it had its perks, but it couldn't be easy. Girls. He was glad he wasn't one.

When they got in the car, it soon became obvious that Chris and Josh had other plans that didn't include a late movie. Chris began to drive too fast. Marco wanted to tell him to slow down, but he felt like everyone would tease him if he said something. Most of all, he didn't want Abigail to think he was a wimp. The car was full, and she was sitting on his lap in the backseat; her long blond hair, which smelled insanely good—was it raspberries?—was pressed pleasantly against his nose. Also, if he said anything, she might move, which he didn't want her to do.

Chris drove them to the Sabine River Bridge. They were looking up at Houston's skyline, sitting on a ledge over the Buffalo
Bayou. It made Marco think of Buenos Aires and home. Lily. He
hadn't texted her to let her know he was safe.

"Do you smoke?" Abigail was rooting around in her glossy,
oversized orange bag. Marco laughed.

"No way!" he said, wrinkling his nose as Abigail removed a
box of cigarettes from her purse and lit one. "That is disgusting,"
he said, pointing to the lit cigarette.

"I agree," said Emily.

"Toss me one," said Josh.

"Man, do it. It will make it easier for Marco and me to clean
up the basketball court with your sorry ass next week," Chris said.

"Oh yeah, and that beer you're about to open is going to
make you eligible for the Olympics!" Josh said.

"This? This just makes you fat. That"—Chris pointed to Josh's
now-lit cigarette—"that will kill you dead."

"Can we talk about something else? This is depressing. I really
wanted to see the movie," Emily said.

"What movie were we going to see?" Marco asked her.

"*Iron Man 3.*"

"Oh! You guys totally suck. Do you know how long it takes for
movies to get to Buenos Aires?" Marco said to Chris and Josh.

The two boys held their hands up. "Don't look at us. This was
her idea." They were looking at Abigail.

"This is more fun. Look at those stars. And, Marco, if you don't
like the smoke, I won't smoke around you," she said, stabbing out
her cigarette. Josh and Chris made kissing noises. Marco admon-
ished them in Spanish.

"Dude, you know I don't speak Buenos Aires," Chris said.
Marco laughed.

"You're such an ass." Marco lurched at Chris playfully, and the two started to wrestle.

"Marco, come take a walk with me. I want to show you something really cool near the water tower," Abigail said.

"Better go, Dude. Good luck," Chris said.

Marco could hear Emily as he and Abigail walked away from their small party. "I hate it when she does this." Marco heard Josh say to her, "Have another beer," before Abigail led him down a small path that eventually reached a glen of trees blackened with the darkness of the night. There was a small opening and a big, flat rock that almost looked like a big, stone love seat. Abigail lit the way with her iPhone.

"This is what I wanted to show you!"

"It's cool," Marco said appreciatively. Abigail sat down on the rock and patted the space next to her. She pulled two beers from her bag and passed one to Marco. She opened them with an opener she dug out of her purse.

"What else do you have in there? A small dog and a house-plant?" Marco asked.

"I really like your accent. It's cold! I'm freezing," Abigail said, moving closer to him. Marco felt self-conscious and aroused all in one blow. He didn't drink much, and the beer was going straight to his head, along with Abigail. She took his beer out of his hand and tilted his face down to hers. When their lips touched, he thought he might explode. He had never felt this sort of searing attraction. In moments, she was fumbling with his belt buckle.

"Whoa, slow down," Marco heard himself say.

"What?" Abigail said, surprised.

"I've had a long day, flight..." Marco fumbled.

"And..." Abigail looked at him in the darkness.

It was a good question. Why was he stopping this gorgeous girl from living out many a late-night fantasy? It just felt too fast.

Too strange. Part of him wanted to just grab her and go for it, but his mind was warring with that part. Lily would be devastated. Dammit. She was *not* his girlfriend. But he cared about her feelings. But Abigail was just so different—so smooth, so slick, so utterly different. And to be honest, so white and rich and Texan. She was intoxicating. Marco was reminded of too much ice cream or candy or soda.

"I get it. You want to take it slow. That's really adorable."

"Are you making fun of me again?"

"When did I make fun of you before?" Abigail said, shocked.

"My accent...about five minutes ago..." Marco said.

"Listen, I wasn't making fun of you then, and I'm not now. We'll take it slow. I can do that. That is, if you want to take it at all..." Abigail said, sounding more sincere than she had all night.

"I do. How about that movie tomorrow night?" Marco asked, drawing her onto his lap for another kiss.

"Sounds great." Marco could feel her smiling through their softer kisses.

"We'd better get back."

"Let's go." The two held hands as they walked back toward their friends.

SEVENTEEN

Marco's head hurt. Bad. He simply didn't drink alcohol, and he had ended up having three beers last night. His tongue felt heavy and disgusting. He wanted to go back to sleep, but he was too thirsty, and his head hurt too much. He had no experience with hangovers and had no idea what to do to relieve this state of total discomfort. He kicked the covers aside and rolled out of bed. Standing up made things worse. He ran to the bathroom, eager to vomit the alcohol out of his system, but he had no luck. Defeated, he brushed his teeth, splashed ice-cold water on his face, and headed downstairs to the kitchen where he found Jim seated at the island, reading the newspaper.

"You look like crap," Jim said matter-of-factly. Marco answered in Spanish that he did indeed feel like crap. Jim told him to sit, which Marco did without complaint. Jim began pulling things from the refrigerator—a carton of eggs, a wedge of white cheddar cheese, some butter, and a carton of orange juice. He poured Marco a tall glass of ice water while simultaneously pulling a loaf of bread from a drawer. When Marco finished the water, grateful for its cooling effect on both his head and his throat, Jim spoke.

"Want to tell me what happened last night?" As he said this, he tossed Marco a bottle of pain medicine from the cabinet.

"I'm not really sure," Marco said honestly. He certainly hadn't consumed enough to black out, nothing like that. It was just hard to conjure Abigail's effect on him when she wasn't actually there in the room.

"How much did you have to drink?" Jim asked as he cracked several eggs, impressively with one hand, into a large glass bowl. He whisked them into a fluff and dumped a handful of grated cheese into the bowl. "This will fix you up, by the way."

"Thank you. I don't usually drink. I had maybe three beers," Marco said.

"If three beers put you into this shape, I think it is safe to say you don't drink much. That's good. Stick with that. So what happened last night?" Jim sliced a pat of butter and dropped it into a frying pan, where it sizzled up at him in response. "Mmm, I never eat like this anymore. This is going to be delicious."

"I'm not sure if I can eat," Marco said, eyeing the frying pan doubtfully and avoiding Jim's question for the moment. He didn't know exactly what had happened, and his head hurt too much to think about it. "Is there any coffee?" Jim motioned to the coffeemaker with his chin while he slid the omelet onto a plate. The toaster pinged at the same moment, and slices of toast popped up with enthusiasm.

Marco stared at the strange coffee machine and its coffee pods. He groaned. He just wanted a cup of coffee.

"I'll get that," Jim said, coming to his rescue. "You get started on that." Jim pointed to an impressive plate of food he had whipped up almost magically.

"How long have I been staring at that coffee maker?" Marco thought to himself.

Jim was right. The food tasted delicious. "It's the grease; it absorbs the alcohol," Jim said, pointing his fork at Marco's almost-empty plate. Marco thought of his pals at school and how they always wanted a huge, greasy breakfast of potatoes and eggs after a big night out. Made sense now. Marco himself didn't drink because of sports. He believed it would ruin his endurance and make him fat.

"I feel weird talking about last night," Marco finally said, honestly. He had never spoken to Jim about girls. Part of him wanted to tell Jim everything about Lily and Abigail—it would be a relief of sorts. Marco was the type of person who kept things to himself. He remembered he used to confide in his mother. The thought of her brought on a quick jab of sadness. Marco cleared his throat to remove the feeling.

"Abigail is a pretty girl," Jim said, as if reading Marco's thoughts. Jim was trying to give Marco an entry point, and Marco appreciated his efforts.

"Maybe too pretty," Marco said, finishing his coffee.

"Ah. Does she like one of the other guys?" Jim said, misunderstanding.

"Nah, it's not that. She's just, well, different. Faster," Marco said.

"Oh, I see," Jim said, surprised and slightly embarrassed. He quickly recovered. "Was she the reason you were drinking last night?"

"Kind of," Marco said. Marco didn't want Jim to know Abigail smoked. Jim was hugely against smoking. He might never let her in the house again.

"She took me off guard," Marco said plainly, almost more to himself than Jim.

"I don't want you out drinking while you're here, Marco. That's not going to be acceptable to me or to Anita. You are our responsibility..."

"Absolutely, Jim. I'm sorry..."

"You don't have to be sorry, Marco. Everybody screws up. You're just a kid. But be careful with this girl."

"We're going to a movie tonight. If that's all right."

"As long as it's an early one and all you drink is water."

"Yes and yes," Marco said sincerely.

"We've got work tomorrow."

"Tomorrow?" Marco said, surprised.

"Yep. So get to bed early. Idle hands and all that." Jim began to clear the plates when Maria came in.

"I'll get those, Mr. Swanson."

"Thanks, Maria."

Maria and Marco said their proper hellos. They hadn't really had a chance to catch up the night before. Marco loved Jim and Anita, but he was closest to Maria. Maria Gomez was a short, plump, hard-as-hell-working housekeeper for the Swansons. They no longer *needed* her every day, but as long as she wanted the job, according to Jim, it was hers.

Apparently Jim had met Maria when his kids were young. She would clean his office late at night, while Jim was still knocking out the hours, and he'd speak his poor Spanish with her, wishing her well and thanking her for her work. When they lost their housekeeper, Jim asked Maria whether she'd like a day job. She very much had wanted a day job and had been part of the family ever since. With three kids, Anita had been thrilled with the help, and soon Maria became indispensable. These days she was older and in poorer health, but she still worked for the Swansons every day.

Marco and Maria were tight. They shared, after all, a kindred spirit. He saw his own mother in her. Hardworking, uneducated, good-hearted, and caring were the qualities he remembered most about his mother and that he saw in Maria. When he was with Maria, he felt as much at home as anywhere. Being with her brought back memories of working at the church with his mother, and he imagined that if she were still alive, this might be what she would be doing today—cleaning in some rich family's house or estancia to make a living.

After breakfast and a dip in the pool, Marco was feeling much better. Jim took him out for a driving lesson. Last year while he was in the States, he'd begun taking driver's education classes. This year, he'd complete the process to get a Texas driver's permit. Some of his American buddies, like Chris, were driving now, so he'd probably get out a lot, especially during the Thanksgiving and Christmas breaks when his buddies were out of school.

Abigail showed up promptly at five o'clock. They were going to an early movie so Marco could be rested up for work with Jim the next morning. She was like a different girl: no makeup, her hair pulled neatly back into a ponytail, jeans, a sweater, and clean white sneakers. Her energy was different too—less aggressive. When they were about to leave for the movie, Marco's cell phone chimed with an incoming text. It was Lily.

"Did you arrive safe?" it asked.

Marco stared at the screen for a moment, aware of Abigail's eyes on him. She was waiting patiently, but Marco felt as awkward as if the two girls had been there in the same room, both waiting for him. He felt rushed and didn't quite know what to write, so he hit Ignore.

"Let's go." He smiled at Abigail, opening the Swansons' expansive front door for her.

"Is everything all right?" she asked sweetly.

"Everything is great."

EIGHTEEN

Marco tapped his toes somewhat impatiently. Jim was being featured in the *Houston Chronicle's* new Sunday magazine, and somehow between the reporter's schedule and, more to the point, Jim's, the interview couldn't be held until now—four o'clock on Christmas Eve. Marco had wanted to take the bus home to take a nap and get ready for Abigail's parents' annual Christmas party, but Jim had sat him down in one of the conference room's leather swivel chairs. "We'll get there. Have a seat. You might learn something," he said. Jim wanted Marco to hear what he had to say. The Swansons would be attending the party as well, not necessarily because their kids were dating, although there was that, but because both families ran closely in the same social circles.

While the reporter set up his recorder and arranged himself, Marco spun around in the chair, taking in the emptied out office through the glass walls of the conference room. From here he could see the large, open bullpen, where analysts and associates were normally frantically working on spreadsheets and crunching numbers. Now, with everyone gone home, it was as if the market had crashed. The Christmas decorations looked sad without the normal hustle and bustle of the day.

"Do you need anything?" Jim asked the reporter, who was a young man in his twenties named Jack Hartgens. He wore a wrinkled blazer and a tired, intelligent look beneath his expensive eyeglasses. Marco straightened in his chair. He wanted to get out of here, but he didn't want to be rude to the two men. He patted his own coat pocket. A small turquoise Tiffany & Co. box with a white satin bow containing a modest silver necklace for Abigail was nestled in his pocket. He felt both terrified and exhilarated by its presence. It was part of his agitation. Was it too much? Would she like it? It was a silver key. He never said it out loud, but when he saw it, he knew it was perfect. She had unlocked the key to his heart. No, he would never say that—too corny. But it was true. The last three weeks had been unreal. She came skiing with him and the Swansons on their annual ski trip to Vail, where he had sneaked into Abigail's room each night after everyone retired to sleep, and they had kissed, made out, and slept in each other's arms until dawn, when he had tiptoed back to his room. He'd never had so little sleep in his life. He accompanied her on Christmas shopping trips, and she faithfully watched his basketball games, with Emily at her side much of the time. Jim paid him a pretty decent wage for the two days a week he worked, and Marco was able to take Abigail out on modest dates.

When he had first arrived, Marco received long, spirited e-mails from Lily, filled with news from home, but he would only respond with a few brief lines. He felt cruel, but he hadn't told Lily about Abigail—and he usually told Lily everything—and he felt like he was lying to her. But he just couldn't bring himself to tell that truth.

"I spent nearly two decades at Solomon. It was electric." Jim's voice pulled Marco back into the room. "Truth be told, there are only so many years you can do that kind of work. It's a young man's game." The reporter was listening thoughtfully. "So I came to a fork in the road. On the one hand, I could leave and see what else the game held for me, or I could stay at Solomon and not push the envelope. Play it safe and finish my days there. I chose to open my own firm, and here we are." The reporter cleared his throat and started to ask another question, but Jim stopped him.

"Listen, yes, opening my own shop was my second career in a way, but that's not what I want to focus on today."

"OK." The reporter sat up a little straighter.

"I have made a lot of money in my time. Traveled the world, seen some things. We've advised on some notable deals and helped some families sell some marquee franchises. Some would say I've had the world by the tail. And that's all great. But six years ago, I met that young man, and that's when the real accomplishment of my life began." Jim was looking at Marco and smiling broadly. The reporter looked at Marco, and Marco raised his eyebrows in response.

"Relationships. That's what it's all about. I did not get that until the last few years. I'm being really transparent with you here, son." Marco wasn't sure if Jim was speaking to the reporter or himself.

"I'm not sure I am following you, Mr. Swanson," the reporter said.

"Call me Jim."

"Jim."

"Part of the reason I agreed to this interview today is that I want to get a message out there. And I think the holiday season is the perfect time to do it."

"OK..."

"Life is about relationships."

Marco coughed. He felt uncomfortable. He wasn't sure where Jim was going with this. He almost seemed drunk.

"I just didn't see that when I was young and ambitious. My dad didn't see it when I was a child. Men just aren't taught the importance of this. The models of masculinity have to be rejiggered." The reporter looked agog. "I have regrets. I was too obsessed with work when my own kids were young. This business is cut-throat, and all of us have to claw our way up. But that leaves most of us feeling empty. Isolated. There you are in your golden castle, surrounded by money, and your kids can barely stand being in the same room with you," Jim said.

"Is that how your kids feel about you?"

"Come on, Jack. I picked you for this story because I know you are smarter than that."

"You're right, Jim."

"Look, I've built this great practice, and it has become a liveli-hood for a number of employees. At this point, instead of running hard for the next deal, I have the luxury to focus on mentoring, encouraging, and developing my staff so that they can reach their own career goals. Look, I'm not going to say I don't keep a very watchful eye, but my focus has shifted."

"How does that change the climate of the office?"

Jim nodded. "It's a nicer place to work. Ask him," Jim said, gesturing toward Marco.

The reporter shifted his attention toward Marco. "What's your full name? What do you do here?"

"I'm an intern. I'm still in school."

"From your time here, is this what you want to do with your life?"

"No, man. I want to play soccer professionally," Marco said with charming honesty. The two older men laughed at this.

"Stick with that. So, Jim. You probably have some more time on your hands, so is retirement pending? What's on the horizon?" the reporter asked. Jim looked thoughtful at this question. Marco felt a small pang. What would Jim do when he retired? He and Anita barely ever hung out from what he had seen during the last month.

"I'm spending a lot of time at my ranch these days. I've got some thoughts...stay tuned."

The interviewed carried on. Jim moved through his approach to leadership and talked about how great teams could achieve great success. He rattled off all kinds of adages, which had Jack noting these sound bites and imagining how to weave it all into the story. As Jim and Jack wrapped up the interview, saying their holiday well-wishes, Marco remembered the party and the present in his pocket, and all of his anxious agitation returned. He looked at his phone. Things kicked off in three hours.

NINETEEN

They arrived at just past eight. This was River Oaks, where
Houston's old money intermingled with its new wealth in houses
that were more like trophies than homes. In this neighborhood,
houses sat far back from the street down long drives, often with
garages tucked in their backyards. Jim, Anita, and Marco entered
the mansion, which was sparkling with soft white Christmas lights
and had live Christmas music from the string ensemble playing in
the background. Marco peeled off immediately to find his friends
and Abigail.

As the night carried on, Jim and Anita moseyed around the
house, chatting here and there. It was a little past ten: late enough
for the drinkers to have put a few away, but early enough that the
crowd was still full. As usual, Jim drank little. He still liked wine
but never had more than one or two glasses. At sixty-one, he was
still running, biking, and swimming, so he watched how much he
drank. Marco suddenly sauntered up to him, looking happy.

"Hey there, Young Fella. Where are your friends?" Jim said.

"They're here. It's about relationships, Jim," Marco said, referring to the interview earlier that evening. "You and I need to spend
some quality time together."

"You're a punk. You know that, right?"

"I do." Marco smiled. Jim noticed how happy and relaxed Marco looked. Things with Abigail must really be going well.

The two men wandered into the home's library. It was a very masculine room, and there were three men sitting in big chairs. These were powerful men: One was Abigail's father, a managing partner at the largest Houston-based law firm. Another was the son of an oil legend who'd inherited a few hundred million bucks and, as they say, was born on third and thought he'd hit a triple. The final man was a long-standing state senator whose construction company had coincidentally grown huge during the same time that the senator served in the Texas legislature.

"Hey, Jim, come on in here and sit down! We're talking problems and how we bring peace, love, and tranquility to the world."

As they entered, Jim said, "Do you guys all know Marco?" Jim introduced Marco as he always did. "Marco is a good family friend who comes to America as an exchange student every year. He's been visiting us since he was eleven."

Of course, it did not do the relationship justice, but there was never any mention of the financial support or the deeper relationship Marco held with the Swanson family. Close friends knew their story, and that was how they intended to leave it. They had come together through deep tragedy, and it was nobody's business but their own.

"Sure. Sit down, young man, and join us big boys," one man said. As Marco entered, he shook everyone's hand and then grabbed a seat on the sofa along with Jim. He had met Abigail's dad one time before. He was never around.

So, these were the big boys, Marco thought. Jim was a good guy, but Marco had never really sat with a bunch of American men. Jim made the rounds to explain to Marco who each man was and what he did. He didn't understand all of it, but he did understand these were important men. It made him think of Señor Segrato. He'd never met his namesake, but he imagined him to be like these men—rich, powerful, and influential.

The men were loud and obnoxious. Jim sat smiling at times and laughing at other times. He was enjoying the entertainment. Inside Jim thought these guys were OK, but he also thought they were a little too big for their britches. At the end of the day, money did that to people, and these guys were all about the money—the money and the power. And so the conversation continued.

First they were talking about the tax rate and the federal budget. "The Greeks are screwed! They spent too much, raised taxes too much, and now look at them. Sure, it's a nice place to live, and the weather is great. But God! Who is ever going to bring a new job to Greece?" the senator said. Jim wondered whether Marco was regretting choosing this bonding time. He probably wished he was back in the swing of things with his friends.

The lawyer was fat and wore dark glasses; he leaned in with his big arms, swinging his hands around as if to magnify his already loud voice. "Then there are the *C* states, California and Connecticut; the only thing that could make things worse for them is more spics coming across the borders and attending public schools! The kids get *F*'s. The states are *C*'s, and the budgets are *B*'s...for *broke!*" Everyone was laughing.

Jim felt Marco freeze beside him. Dammit. Jim thought to nudge him to tell him it was all right to leave, but for some reason, he didn't. Maybe Marco wasn't that sensitive. Maybe he had just imagined him taking offense.

The conversation carried on, moving to the war in the Middle East, Syria, and Obama's policies. There remained chaos in Middle East, and tensions were rising as democracies in places like Iraq and Afghanistan struggled against the subversive forces of totalitarianism and regimes such as those of Syria and Iran. It didn't help that fears were rising in regards to nuclear armament of countries that remained singularly focused on getting "the bomb."

Eventually, the conversation found its way to South America. The men were plenty drunk, and Marco hadn't said a word. The third-base runner started going on about South American countries and how big a problem they were.

"Look, we've tried to do business in these places. Our counterparties are always pissed at the costs and burdens the rich have. They feel as if they are being taxed at higher and higher rates to support the growing class of people living off the nation."

Talk turned to a conversation the man had had with a family in Argentina. "The problem the Argentines have is the people. I mean, how can you run a country when half of your people are on the dole and don't want to get off?" This time Jim was sure he felt Marco stiffen. "You have people down there whose parents were on the dole, and now they're on the dole, and they don't want a way out. It's a disaster. It's like a loser state full of whores, drug dealers, cock fighters, and soccer stiffs who haven't worked a day in their lives!"

At this, Jim butted in, in part because of Marco, but also because enough was enough, and he needed to call bullshit on the ramblings.

"Listen, I've spent more time than any of you in South America. You guys are full of shit! The facts are, Argentina, as an example, has a constitution modeled after our own, but they've had so many regime changes, course corrections, and weak governments, going back to the devaluation of their currency in 2001, that they have never really adopted the rule of law." Jim was passionate as he spoke.

"If they did, they'd ensure the kind of motivation we have here. The problem there is that if you have success, it can be too easily taken from you, either by the state or by someone more powerful. Only after they recognize the constitution as supreme and establish the kind of judiciary that has the backbone to fight against the establishment when the law calls for it, will you see the country on a course to its fullest potential." Jim paused and took a breath. "Trust me friends, the whores and the cock fighters are only doing their gigs because there is nothing better to do!"

There were some more laughs, but it was late, so Jim stood up abruptly. "You know I always want to have the last word! We gotta go, guys. Merry Christmas!" He shook each man's hand and wished him good night. Marco was in no mood to shake hands. Jim went to put his hand on Marco's back, but Marco shook him off. He stormed out of the room. Jim and the rest of the men watched him.

"What'd we say?" The senator asked. He shrugged and lit a cigar. "I need another scotch."

Jim returned to the party to look for Marco and Anita. It was time to go home. He found Anita in the kitchen, holding her heels in one hand and talking to Pete Matli. She was smiling up at him in a way that sparked a feeling of jealousy in Jim's gut. There was almost adoration in her gaze. A dark thought crossed his mind. No, she wouldn't. She couldn't. Anita noticed Jim standing there.

"I think my ride is about to turn into a pumpkin," Anita said to Pete. Pete shook Jim's hand and wished him a merry Christmas. Jim felt guilty for thinking anything untoward was happening between Anita and Pete. He kissed the top of her head. She looked up at him.

"What was that for?"

"Just merry Christmas," he said quietly.

"Merry Christmas, Jim," she said back in the same hushed tone.

"What's happened to us?" Jim said, almost more to himself than posing an actual question. Anita didn't say anything at first. Then she took his hand.

"Let's go find the babe."

"Good idea," Jim said, letting Anita lead him toward the center of the party. It seemed nowhere near winding down. "Something just happened. It was upsett—"

"What?" Anita asked. She turned and saw what Jim was seeing. Abigail was dancing with another boy. He was tall and blond, and her hands were draped around his neck, her head against his chest.

"Oh boy," Anita said.

At that moment, Marco walked into the room. The collar of his suit was up, and he looked as if he'd come in from the backyard. He saw Abigail and the other boy. Jim and Anita approached him.

"Let's just go," Marco said, seething quietly. His cheeks were flushed with heat, contrasting with the cold he still carried from being outside moments before. Something made Abigail look up at them. She shook her head and extricated herself from the boy. Jim and Anita froze as Abigail approached them.

"Let's go, please. Now!" Marco stormed off. Abigail looked at Jim, who shrugged his shoulders.

"Maybe just give him some space. It's been a rough night." Abigail seemed about to say something but then seemed to think better of it and nodded her head. Anita glared at her and followed Marco.

TWENTY

As they rode home, it was apparent Marco was deeply upset. Jim was trying to figure out what he was more upset about—Abigail or the conversation in the library or the confluence of the two. Jim had certainly sensed the conversation at the party was offensive, but he didn't think it had cut too deep. But even if it hadn't, seeing his girlfriend slow dancing with another guy would have finished the job. Marco was quiet and distant. Jim wanted to give Marco a little space to recover himself. Anita asked Marco a few questions, but he just responded with grunts. Jim would bring Anita up to speed later—after they got home, but before they fell asleep. "No need to stir the pot any further," he thought.

As they pulled up to their home on South Boulevard, they drove under the porte cochere and through to the back, where the garage and guesthouse were located. As they drove in, Marco, who was in the back, began shaking his head. They all got out of the car. Anita was turning to go upstairs to bed when Marco began to speak.

"What in the world am I doing here?" he asked. Jim and Anita looked at each other. Marco's mind seemed to be racing, and he was getting angrier by the second. Something seemed to be coming home for him as he kept shaking his head.

"I'm a peasant, indigent and alone. You don't really care about me." Tears streamed down his face as he continued. "I'm just your project, something you picked up from the whores and the cock fighters and the soccer players. Something you could dust off and show your rich friends." Marco began to sob with anger. "We helped this peasant boy; aren't we great!"

Jim slowly approached Marco, trying to think about what to say. "Marco, those men meant no harm. They didn't want to offend you or seem rude. They're just fat, old, drunk men talking trash...you know, like a bunch of NBA players getting together... trash talking and trying to be funny," Jim said, feeling lame. Marco stared back at Jim, but his thoughts were obviously elsewhere.

"Listen, let's go in and go to bed. It's late, and we can talk about this tomorrow. We can talk about Abigail, too," Anita said with the warmth only a mother can offer.

"I am not going in."

This surprised Jim. He'd never seen Marco be obstinate. After a second, Jim smiled, trying to lift the mood. "Come on, it's not that big of a deal. Come in and get yourself some ice cream or something. Listen, we've all had our hearts stomped on. It hurts like hell, but it's part of life. And maybe Abigail was with a very old friend or an old boyfriend. Come on. I am tired; I need to go to sleep."

Silence. Jim nodded toward the house, gesturing for Anita to go in. "I'll handle this," he said. Anita looked concerned but agreed. She went to Marco and embraced him before saying good night. Marco accepted her embrace stiffly but said, "Good night, Anita," quietly. When she was gone, Jim tried to appeal to him again.

"Marco, seriously, we need to go in. I don't want to leave you out here, and I want to set the alarm and go to sleep."

"Go ahead, set the alarm. Good idea, some spic might try to break in."

"Marco," Jim said, shaking his head.

"I am not going in," Marco said again. At this point, he began to move around the back of the car to grab his old bike, which was a bit too small for his mature frame.

"Marco! You are not going out now; it is too late, and we need to go in." Now Jim was beginning to get agitated.

Marco ignored him. He pressed the garage door opener and, with no helmet, got on the bike and bolted into the night.

Jim was stunned. As he sat there, he didn't know what to do. At first he had been getting angry because he was losing patience, but now he was both at a loss for words and worse, a loss for thoughts. He sat there for two or three minutes, trying to process what had just happened. He also wondered what he was going to tell Anita. Did he do something wrong? What had just happened, and did he cause a crisis?

He made his way upstairs and told Anita that Marco had left. She immediately panicked. After a few minutes, Jim got her to settle down enough to listen to what had transpired in the library at the party. As he spoke, he kept an ear out for the alarm chime signaling Marco's return. By now it was very late; both he and Anita were very tired, and neither was sure what to do. But it was clear that Anita expected Jim to do *something*.

"Listen, I'll drive around the block and see whether I see him. I'll also leave the back door unlocked, and you call me if you hear the alarm chime. OK?"

Jim grabbed his cell phone, went back to the garage, and got in the car. He made his way out of the driveway and began by driving down their street and then around a few blocks. The streets were quiet and twinkling with the coming of Christmas. Jim had a strange, tired thought: "Could Santa, his sleigh, and his team of reindeer help him right now?"

Jim kept thinking, "Where would the kid go?" At first he thought maybe to a basketball court they played at, but as he passed by it, he saw no light. He kept expanding his range. Time was moving on, and he was getting more tired. He figured the last place he should try was a shopping area several miles from the house that had a lot of nightlife that might attract Marco's attention. As he drove through the Village, as it was known, he saw a lot of young people on bikes. This was near Rice University, and students came over here to the pubs, restaurants, coffee houses, and ice-cream parlors. It was late. The streets were much quieter than usual. Still, no luck. No Marco that he could see.

It was after two when he decided he'd done all he could tonight. Marco was big, responsible, and smart. And maybe he'd already made it home.

As Jim drove home, he went through the neighborhood again, using back streets just to see whether he saw Marco. As he came near his own street, he needed to pass a more prominent thoroughfare. It was late, his eyes were growing more and more heavy, and nothing good was going to happen from this point on. As he crossed the street, he looked left and saw a cop car had pulled someone over. He thought nothing of it.

When Jim got home, he and Anita spoke. He was tired, and while they were both concerned, they'd raised three kids before. Marco was responsible. He was capable of taking care of himself. Through their conversation, they both felt confident he'd return before too long. Jim decided they needed to get some sleep.

They turned out the lights, and Anita snuggled against him. He was surprised by her touch. Normally they said good night and went their separate ways in the expanse of their king-size mattress. But tonight was different, and Jim didn't know whether it was the adrenaline from worrying about Marco, the seduction of Christmas, or something else, but Anita was definitely making a pass at him.

They made love.

It had been years.

Jim felt tears stream down Anita's cheeks as he pressed his face to hers, and somehow he captured their meaning. She was saying good-bye in some way. There was something sad and final about their lovemaking. If Jim hadn't been so tired, he would have made her use words for what was transpiring between them. Years later, he would look back on that night and wish he had turned the light on and made her speak to him. Perhaps he could have drawn her back. She was open to him in that moment, but he had been so tired from the night's events. So tired. And the next day, all hell broke loose.

TWENTY-ONE

Jim woke early, as usual. At first, he began his routine on auto-pilot—eager to read the paper and have his coffee before the Christmas festivities began—but somewhere near the coffee pot, he remembered last night. He rushed back to Marco's room. He was not there. Jim went to the garage, causing the chime to sound, to see whether the bike was there. Anita had stirred all night, and the chime was enough to wake her. As Jim reentered the house having found no bike, the chime sounded again, and Anita called down to him.

He went upstairs and again, with a dumbstruck face, entered the master bedroom. "He's not here; at least I don't see him or the bike," he said.

Anita jumped up again, panic setting in. "What are we going to do?"

At that moment, Jim's face changed. He tensed up. Something was wrong, seriously wrong.

"Jim, what is it?"

Jim dashed to the phone and dialed 911. Anita stared at him, alarmed.

"Yes, my name is Jim Swanson. I live here on South Boulevard. My son is missing, and he has no ID. He is a male, age seventeen, Hispanic, speaks with an accent, and was last seen on his bike last night around midnight…" Jim paused for a brief moment, listening to the operator on the other end of the line.

"Yes, I understand, but there is something else. I don't know whether you can check the records, but I did go looking for him. When I was coming home, about a half mile west of my location, I noticed lights. I thought it was the police pulling a motorist over." Anita gasped and put her hand over her mouth. "It would have been on Bissonnet, near Woodhead. Do you have any record of any pedestrian accident there last night? Yes, I can hold."

"Oh my God," he heard Anita say, but he didn't look at her. Jim's heart was racing.

"Jim, was there a wreck last night?" Anita was out of bed now and pacing. Jim put his hand up to signal for her to wait. He wasn't ignoring her, but she could tell he was totally focused, and his thoughts were moving at ninety miles per hour.

He was good in a crisis. She was not. Her heart was pounding, but after all these years, this was when she needed to let him execute. He was cool, but he was trying to remember in great detail the lights and what he had seen. He continued to wait. He covered the phone with his hand.

"Anita, I think I may have seen an ambulance last night. I mean, when I saw it, I thought it was a cop, but now that I think about it again…Jesus. It might have been a cop and a second emergency vehicle…on Bissonnet…I didn't—" The operator began to speak. Jim stopped talking and listened. Anita was throwing on sweats and racing around the room.

"Yes. Yes. I understand. What should I do now? OK. I can do that. Do you have my information? I need to give you my cell phone, too." Jim hung up the phone and looked into Anita's eyes. She was pacing, frightened and panicked.

"Anita, I think Marco may have been hit by a car last night. Listen to me and repeat back to me what I need you to do. Do you understand?"

"Yes." Anita had stopped pacing and began to slowly move to a chair in the bedroom to sit. In her mind, things were slowing down considerably, and her body showed fear and confusion.

"Good. You need to get up and take a shower. You need to pack some things for Marco and me and be ready to come when I call you. You have some time, so go slow. Be prepared for me to call you and tell you what hospital to come to. Also, call Father Diaz in Buenos Aires, and if you don't get him, send him an e-mail. Tell him that Marco may have been in an accident and that I will call him later..." Jim paused. "Ask him to say a prayer for safety." Jim had tears in his eyes when he said this last part. Anita jumped up from the chair and embraced him. They pulled apart. "Now repeat that back to me."

Jim walked into his bathroom and threw water on his face. He brushed his teeth and put on a pair of slacks, a golf shirt, and some driving loafers. All of this took less than two minutes. He stopped one last time to make sure he had what he needed. On the way out, he grabbed his phone and his tablet. With these two weapons he could get through anything.

Jim got into his Mercedes and began to drive to Ben Taub Hospital. This was the county hospital. While it was not the best hospital in Houston, it *was* best for GSWs (gunshot wounds). It had an exceptional emergency room, and if the boy were seriously injured, he would have been well cared for. But he would have to be moved as soon as possible because it was not a place you wanted to receive posttraumatic care.

As Jim walked into the ER, he had little to go on. The dispatcher could legally offer no information. But Jim sensed she was giving him a hint. She said that given the location he was mentioning, had there been an injured person without ID who needed to be transported to an ER, the EMTs would have likely gone to Ben Taub.

Jim walked into the receiving area, and as was typical, he approached the desk with authority. He was acting as if he had already been notified. "I'll make them believe I already know he is here, and if he's not here, I'll hit Hermann Hospital next," he thought.

"My son was brought here last night at about one or two o'clock in the morning after an accident on his bike...I mean his bicycle. He was hit by a car on Bissonnet. He didn't have any ID, and you probably recorded him as a John Doe," Jim said to the desk attendant.

"I can help you. Let me check the admissions." A young man with glasses and dressed in green nursing scrubs tapped on his keyboard. "Let's see...uh...it's a male. How old is he?" he asked Jim.

Jim launched into full description mode, basically giving too much information. "He's seventeen years old, dark haired, speaks with an accent, and is probably six foot one and about a hundred eighty pounds. He was wearing khaki slacks and a long-sleeved dress shirt, but I am not—"

"Thank you, sir." The young man gave Jim a sympathetic nod. "I just needed his approximate age. I think I have him, but I don't think he was hit by a car."

Jim put his hand to his chest. "Thank God."

"Where did you get that information? I need to verify your identification because this patient is unconscious. Do you have some ID?"

"Unconscious!" Jim's heart was racing. "Where is he? Is he OK? I need to see him." Jim lost his cool.

"Sir, I can help you, but we have a process. So first I need to see some ID. Do you have a driver's license?"

Jim produced his Texas driver's license and tapped his foot anxiously. After a few minutes, which felt like a small eternity, the attendant referred the case to the floor supervisor, who began the process of clearing the ID and contacting the medical team.

Jim learned that Marco had not been struck by a car.

TWENTY-TWO

Marco was trying to wake up.

"Why can't I wake up?" he thought.

He slipped back into a strange, murky ether of dreams that seemed more like thoughts. Clouded. Uncontrollable.

He'd been riding his bike, and he'd been upset. What had he been so upset about? Angry. Sad. Confused. Hopeless.

He couldn't get his thoughts straight. It felt as if something were pressing on his chest.

An image of himself crashing on his bike. He watched the scene from above. The rain. The lights from the oncoming car. The pothole. Too late to see. Too late to recover.

"Did that really happen?"

A couple. Older. Not Jim and Anita. Police cars and ambulances. He needed Jim. He needed Anita. He needed...Abigail.

The Christmas party. Why? What had he done wrong?

"Was this all a bad dream? Why am I always so alone?"

Minutes after Jim had arrived in the ER, he had been briefed on the biking accident and Marco's current condition. Marco had a broken right forearm with a compound fracture, a broken collarbone, several cracked ribs, and a punctured lung, which was impacting his breathing. The medical team had chilled Marco's head to slow down any possible swelling of the brain.

They had taken an MRI, but the results were not yet back. With the labored breathing and the pain medications they provided because of the broken bones, Marco had not yet regained full consciousness.

Now, Jim sat next to Marco's hospital bed, lightly holding Marco's hand. Marco tossed and turned and whimpered and called out for Jim and his friend Lily from Argentina. Jim's heart broke as Marco also called out for his mother in Spanish.

Jim was scared, and a lot of emotions were pouring over him. He was despondent. He felt culpable and convicted. Marco had been right to be angry. He had been right to feel isolated. The conversation at the Christmas party had been out of line, and a better man would have cut it off or challenged the conversation.

Jim had lived in this world of affluent, intelligent, and successful people his whole life. He'd prospered from it and existed in the middle of it. But when you looked deep inside, he hadn't been one of them, or at least he'd always wanted to believe he wasn't. Now he was realizing that if you walk the walk and talk the talk, you are the real deal. Jim was indeed one of them, and it made him sick. Jim prayed, "Just make him OK. I'll change. I'll make this right."

Marco woke that afternoon to Anita and Jim at his side. He was in excruciating pain, and he was not going home anytime soon. In the next two days, there would be two surgeries to help set and pin the bones that were broken. His lung had received a chest tube, a procedure designed to help it reinflate.

The broken ribs and collapsed lung made every breath a challenge and brought terrible pain. He had a button he could punch to administer more pain medicine, but it was of little help. For Marco, it was all a blur. In his waking moments, he revisited complex, painful emotions that he needed time to sort out and articulate. Jim cleared his schedule and remained faithfully by Marco's side. Anita came daily with food and things from home to make Marco more comfortable.

The pain and the recovery left Marco feeling depressed, inadequate, and insecure. Of the visitors who trailed in and out to see him—Chris, Josh, and even Emily—Abigail was not one of them. Along with mending his body, he was nursing a broken heart. Jim and Anita wished they could trade places with him.

As Marco convalesced, hope began to drift in, and he began to organize his thoughts. Through this process, he realized he had come to a sort of crossroads, and there were things, however painful, he needed to say to Jim. Sometime during the second week of his stay in the hospital, the conversation occurred.

"Am I your project?" Marco asked out of the blue.

Marco was in bed, and Jim was in a chair next to the bed, clearing e-mails from his Blackberry. He spent his days working on his Blackberry, reading work materials or magazines, and periodically stepping out to make phone calls. Most days were filled with long periods of silence. Quickly bored with the TV, Marco often just sat silently.

"Huh?" Jim wasn't really paying attention. "What do you mean?" As Jim replied, he considered the question. Before Marco could answer, Jim began to believe he knew where this was going.

"You rich Americans help some poor bastard and feel as if you are doing some great justice, and yet you blame all of the problems of the world on the poor people. It's like this is a bunch of lies." Marco used his arm to gesture at the room around him. His words had contained more venom than he intended, but the sentiment was there. He needed to get this out. "I mean, I get it that there are people who rely on a welfare state to provide for them, but they often have no way to advance or improve their circumstances. The rich and powerful use their positions to hoard and possess and compound, but they do not often provide opportunity to others because it takes from their own success."

There was a long silence.

"I don't want to be your project. I'll take care of myself. I wanted to leave your mansion and be somewhere else so bad...I want to be home now. Home in Argentina, where my people are, where I can live with the poor people." Marco took a labored breath. Jim stood up to make sure he was OK. Marco held up his hand to stop him.

"I don't want to be at a boarding school where the rich kids talk behind my back and blame me and my kind for the problems in my country. I come here, and all I hear from you and your friends is that people like me are the reason for the world's problems. You and your friends suck!"

There was again a long silence.

"They are not my friends, Marco," Jim said quietly as he felt the sting of remorse and pain of having hurt someone he loved very much.

"That's a cop-out, Jim. I'm not letting you off the hook so easily." Jim raised his eyebrows in surprise. He wasn't angry, just surprised at how smart and assertive Marco had become. It was really remarkable.

"You're right, Marco. I have been thinking the very same thing since the night of the accident."

"Good," Marco said, obviously pleased with himself. Jim didn't respond out of respect. Let the young man have his moment. "Where are my clothes? The ones from the night of the accident?"

"Hmm," Jim said, surprised by the turn in conversation. "Wait, why? You're not planning on going anywhere, right?" Marco laughed at this. He wasn't exactly in a position to walk out of there.

"No," Marco said quietly.

"Listen, Marco. I've made some mistakes in my life. I've been doing a lot of soul searching. I thought I had things pretty well figured out lately, but you've made me see I have a long way to go…" Jim paused, smiling to himself. "Funny how life is like that. Anyway, I hope you'll stay. You're a young man now, and it is your choice, but I do hope you'll stay and give me the chance to make things up to you." As Jim said this, he slapped his knees and stood up. There was a small wardrobe in the hospital room where he found Marco's torn-up dress clothes from Christmas Eve and a small plastic bag. Jim held up the bag. Marco gestured for him to bring it over.

Marco removed, to Jim's surprise, a small Tiffany & Co. gift box. Jim held his breath, thinking, "Marco could not have been proposing to Abigail that night? Was that why he was so upset?"

"It's not what you are thinking, Jim," Marco said without looking up. He handed the box to Jim. "Open it."

Jim furrowed his brows. "This seems very personal, Marco."

"It's meaningless."

Not knowing what else to say, Jim untied the satin ribbon and lifted the small lid off of the box. He removed the necklace from its tiny robin's-egg-blue suede envelope.

"It's lovely, Marco."

"She never got to see it."

Jim was silent in response. He had wondered what had happened with Abigail, but he was old enough to know people could go hot and cold like that on you. That was definitely one of life's harder lessons.

"I think I was her project, too," Marco said soberly.

"Marco—"

"It's true. She was never going to be serious about me, was she?"

Jim thought about Abigail's father and her family. Sadly, Marco was probably right. Talk about insult to injury. Before Jim could answer, Marco spoke.

"Jim, can I use your phone?"

"Of course." Marco's phone had gotten smashed in the accident. "I'll get you another iPhone..." Jim paused. "If that's OK with you," he said tentatively.

"It's OK." Marco nodded, smiling. "How about a first-class ticket home in January, too?"

"Now you're pushing it, Mister." Jim laughed, relieved that the air was lighter between them.

"OK, OK." Marco held his hands up. "Ow! It hurts to laugh." Jim handed him the phone. "May I have some privacy?" Marco asked sincerely.

"Of course! I'll go get some coffee." As Jim walked out of the room, he heard Marco say, "Lily? It's Marco. Can we talk?"

TWENTY-THREE

Jim stayed in the hospital almost full-time. He and Anita had leveraged nannies for raising their kids with great success, but it had left Jim empty. He loved his kids, and they loved him, but at over sixty years old, he was more focused on his purpose. And right now, his purpose was to see Marco through recovery.

As the hours turned into days, Jim began to contemplate how the accident might impact Marco's plans. He had come to the States this time, in part, to complete his Eagle Scout project. It was a lot to do, and they'd been working on it, but the time had come for the real work. Now, with his injuries, Marco would not be able to complete the project as planned.

While Marco was recuperating, Jim was working with the troop and the area council, whose office was involved in approving Eagle Scout projects. Together, they were considering alternative strategies for Marco. An Eagle project had to be completed before the scout turned eighteen. This would be Marco's last time in the States before his eighteenth birthday. And the rules were clear: the scout had to complete the project himself. However, in most cases, the projects required additional volunteers. Younger scouts received service hours that counted toward their own advancement for working on these projects. When they helped out, their parents often lent a hand, too.

There was an agreement between the leaders involved that outlined the scope of the project's program and that permitted Jim, as a volunteer, to help organize some of the scheduling, given Marco's current medical status. These were things Marco should be doing, but all involved felt that as long as Marco were present during the hours while the crew worked, then the troop and the council would be satisfied the work was done adequately and met the standards required.

Marco's project was to plant over one thousand saplings in Memorial Park. Years earlier, over 30 percent of the trees within the park had perished in a terrible drought. Most affected were pine trees and oaks. The conditions had been devastating to the city of Houston. What had once been some of the most beautiful urban woodlands in the state were now sparse and thin.

After raising money and getting donations, the team would work through a section of the park, planting half- and one-gallon trees, fertilizing the soil after planting, and praying for the rain. The drought's devastation hit hardest in 2011 and lasted a few more years after that. Tree planting had become a great restoration effort for Eagle Scouts all across the state. Organizations like Trees for Houston welcomed the labor and effort, providing resources and fundraising subsidies for these types of projects. The scouts got to give back to the outdoors, which is an important component of the scouting program, and in doing so, they revitalized communities and the environment.

Within days of Marco's accident, Jim had connected with Marco's American buddies. He also contacted both the church where Marco was raised and the boarding school he attended. The message of his accident was spreading among his friends in Argentina, too. Whatever Marco was feeling these days about his place in the world, the facts were that many considered him a great guy. Sure, some people had said things in front of and behind his back, but his friends defended him, loved him, and supported him.

Marco received notes and cards from the school friends and visits from his basketball and scout buddies in the States consistently throughout his stay in the hospital. Their presence helped bring him joy and raise his spirits. After they'd leave, Jim and Marco would engage in conversation, and the more friends came, the more healing occurred. Jim used this time to reinforce his and Anita's true feelings for Marco. Not only did he share with the boy how much they loved him, but also that they considered him to be a great blessing to them. Since it was Christmas break, a lot of guys spent time hanging with him at the hospital once Marco was up for it.

Behind the scenes, Jim was focused on getting the project ready. News came that a group of school friends were going to fly in from their own South American summer vacations in Argentina to help out. Marco's project plan called for a crew of five to ten scouts to work over two to three days planting the trees. Jim couldn't help himself. Once Marco opened up about his friendship with Lily, Jim made sure she would be among the Argentine crew to visit Marco.

As the day approached, Jim outlined some of the legwork he'd been doing. He approached it as if he were reporting to a boss. He said things like, "I think today you might need to make a call to the Parks Department; would you like me to knock that out for you if you have some friends coming over?" Jim and Marco began to organize in greater detail, but some things Jim held back. Given the accident and the conversation that followed, Jim wanted to help Marco see the amount of love his friends had for him. He was pretty shocked that Abigail had not even once called Marco, but again, life could be cruel. He and Marco certainly knew that. It truly seemed that sometimes those with the most money had the least amount of integrity.

Jim worked hard promoting the project. The troop agreed to make it a priority, and since it was a large troop, they hoped to have a lot of scouts involved. Marco's closest friends in the troop treated the project like a surprise birthday party and were certain to play it down.

"Yeah, I'll be there, Man, but I can't stay all day...I'll talk to some other guys...we'll help, but I don't know, Man, a thousand trees is a lot!" With a crew coming from South America, Jim knew he was going to need more trees. With a little money, a few calls to the Parks Department, and some connections within the city's elite, he set his sights on something far greater than Marco had originally planned. In the second week of January, Marco was released from the hospital.

TWENTY-FOUR

Marco and Jim woke early on January 15. It was a Saturday and the first day of the project. Marco was moving slowly and used a wheelchair for long distances. They planned on moving him out to the site in the park where the scouts were supposed to meet.

Marco knew he would direct the crew, but since he hadn't been able to put much effort into the project during these last few weeks, he didn't think many would show. He was not looking forward to the day ahead, but he knew he had an obligation. He was also not certain he would attain the Eagle rank, but he kept this quiet. Jim, as always, was optimistic and encouraged Marco to just at least stick to the plan—casts, braces, and all.

As they drove into Memorial Park, there were a lot of runners and Saturday morning visitors. Marco watched anxiously, searching for people he knew, as crowds of runners and fitness people gathered at different locations. He saw a group near where they were parking and also several City of Houston Parks Department vehicles, but he thought nothing of it. He kept looking for some of the things he was expecting and his few buddies. Trees and supplies were to be delivered, and he hadn't spotted any scouts yet.

Jim kept quiet. After they parked, he got Marco's wheelchair out and encouraged him to ride in it at first, because they would be covering a lot of ground. It was just before nine. As Jim pushed

Marco toward the big city trucks, Marco thought they were passing a construction site. "Perhaps they are repairing a parking lot," he thought.

Once on the other side of the trucks, Marco gasped.

There were over fifty volunteers, some in their scout uniforms and some in work clothes.

Marco was stunned. Ten of his school buddies from Argentina came over first to greet him. He was speechless. They spoke in Spanish for a long time, asking Marco how he was, telling him that they knew all about the accident.

And then came Lily. She was dressed in jeans, with her hair pulled into a bun and a huge grin. She and Marco hugged for a long time.

"I'm an asshole," he said, his eyes watering.

"Well, you are. But you're my best friend, and I'll take you, warts and all."

The Argentine teens and the American teens were fast friends. One and all were there because they loved Marco and were excited to help. They were pumped to see all of the effort and were blown away with how big of a project this was.

As they were talking and complimenting Marco, Marco himself was trying to do some mental math. Why were all of these people here? This certainly was more than his project called for.

After a few minutes, Jim made eye contact with Marco.

"Marco, I've been holding something back. We've been using your project plan to increase the scope of what you wanted to do. Everything is how you originally outlined it; it's just that we have a few more supplies and people."

"I'd say so," Marco said tentatively.

"Your buddies came from Argentina to lend a hand, but you need to get this thing going. Your senior patrol leader has done a few things to get the first steps in place, but everyone is over there waiting for you." Jim put his hand on Marco's shoulder.

"I'll be around, but this is your show. There are over five thousand trees to be planted, so you need to get these people working!" Jim smiled. "Since they'll be working in different areas of the park, I'll drive you around as needed. But right now, they need your instructions. Do you want me to push you over, or do you want to walk?"

"Move aside, old man," Marco said. Jim feigned shock and hurt, putting his hand to his chest. Marco was excited! "I'll walk!" Marco said, as he made a very gallant and successful effort to stand. Jim knew that it couldn't have been easy and admired Marco for the effort even more than he already did, if that were possible.

Jim faded into the background. The Argentines helped Marco get around, and as he got to the crowd, there was a burst of applause. A kid from the crowd said, "Hey, Marco, what do you want me to do?"

Marco raised his hand and thanked everyone for coming. Then he repeated himself in Spanish and thanked his friends from school. He told them what he wanted to accomplish, and during his instructions, he got a little help from the troop's senior patrol leader. The scout indicated the things that had already been done, and when Marco gave an instruction that still needed to happen, he helped the volunteers get started. Marco was in charge, but the troop's existing command structure was executing his plan on an exponentially bigger scale.

The day moved along with remarkable smoothness. The Parks Department had several heavy vehicles there, and as Marco directed, they moved supplies. Despite how the project had mushroomed, there was relatively good coordination between his instructions and what they had anticipated.

During the day, Marco was moved through the park to different sites where groups were working. Slowly, small trees were popping up all through the sparse land. A local news crew visited, and a newspaper reporter and a photographer arrived for a quick interview. Marco enjoyed the attention, and by the end of the day, the entire project was complete.

It was a huge success.

Marco's project even made that evening's news, and within the week, the local section of the newspaper ran a story about it.

TWENTY-FIVE

Marco was nervous. He was not used to speaking in front of a crowd. Jim was speaking at the moment, and Marco was next.

Lily sat next to Marco. She was dressed in one of Anita's dresses, which was a simple cut and a pretty shade of blue. She looked beautiful. They held hands under the table, but purely as friends. Lily had changed over the summer. She had rules—no kissing, no cuddling.

Just friends.

She and Marco's other pals from Argentina who had flown in to help with the project had stayed on for a few days with the Swansons. For some, including Lily, it was their first time in the States. It was a blast having them there. Marco couldn't think of anything better than having all of his peeps in one place.

Tonight was Marco's Eagle court of honor. Jim had wanted to make sure Marco's success was celebrated while his friends from Argentina were still in Houston. They were in the Grand Hall of the church that sponsored Marco's troop. These celebrations were significant events that drew most of the scouts participating in the organization and their families. The scouts attended in their class A uniforms, including their scout pants and patch-filled shirts, with red neckerchiefs drooping in triangles over their shoulders. Adult leaders also wore their uniforms, and others were wearing dress clothes, as Jim was.

Marco, too, wore his best uniform with his neckerchief and a sash across his torso. On the sash were patches for each of the many merit badges he'd earned over the years. On his shirt above his heart was the Life Scout patch, signifying the rank just before Eagle. Tonight, this would be permanently replaced by the highest achievement in scouting and perhaps the most recognized accomplishment of all youth organizations worldwide. Attaining Eagle Scout was neither easy nor trivial, which is why it remained a significant lifetime achievement.

Jim was coming to the end of his speech. Marco was listening and was deeply touched by Jim's stories about their years in the scouts together. There were fun, jovial stories about their adventures camping and the like, but as Jim neared the end of the speech, his words became more personal, more emotional.

"Marco's presence has changed my life...It is through this young man's eyes, this fine, fine young man..."—Jim wiped a tear from his eyes. Marco forgot all about his nervousness as Jim looked out at him from the podium—"that I have come to see the world from a different perspective. A more human perspective." Anita smiled at Marco from across the table. She winked at Lily. Jim continued.

"Marco, Anita and I want to thank you for the time you've been a part of our lives and our family. We are proud of you and know that your future remains bright. Do not waver, stay on the course you are called to be on, and trust your instincts and judgment and"—this part Marco mouthed with Jim as he said the words—"you can change the world." Marco and Jim were locked eye to eye.

"I also want you to know that I am humbled every day to have been given the privilege of knowing you. You have literally transformed me each year you've visited. Not only do I love you as I have each one of my own children, but I am also grateful that you have shown me some things about my own life that needed changing." Jim nodded his head. "And these changes have left me transformed for the better." Marco nodded his own head in response. "This year was a scary year, but through these trials, I have learned more about what I should be doing in my own life than perhaps I learned in my entire career. Thank you for that." Jim closed to a hearty round of applause from the audience. Anita kissed him on the cheek when he sat back down at the table where Marco and Lily were seated.

Marco rose to speak. His nerves were back. "You can do it," said Lily encouragingly. Anita and Jim liked Lily. She was down-to-earth, grounded.

The troop leader pinned Marco with his Eagle Badge and stepped aside for Marco to speak. Marco took a deep breath and cleared his throat. When he began to speak, he found it was much easier than he had expected. Jim and Anita noted that he was a natural.

"Wow. This kid should be in politics!" Anita said, a bit thrilled by the surprising gravity of Marco's presence at the podium.

"I was not born to stand before you today. I was not born to live a life summering in Houston." The audience laughed, and Jim raised his eyebrows. He too was impressed. Marco became more serious. "I was not born to be educated, let alone educated in one of my country's finest elite schools. I was not born to be in *front* of any crowd, let alone standing above you on a podium with any right to speak with authority. I was not born to be comfortable or to be affluent. And I certainly was not born to be an Eagle Scout..." Marco paused. He had the crowd wrapped around his finger.

"And yet, I am told, and remember in some ways, that my mother would have given all she had and more to see that these things might indeed be true for me. I have no belongings and no money. But this much I have learned in the past few weeks: I have more than I could ever have wished for. I see you here in this room as my family, and I count my friendships with you as blessings beyond my imagination." Marco remained calm and clear minded, while everyone else in the room was choking up.

"I now know that all my mother might have prayed for or asked for, all that she would have worked for to provide a better life for me, is indeed here in this room with all of you. Thank you for all you have done for me, and thank you for this opportunity to be one more in the line of many great Eagle Scouts in our troop. And thank you to Anita and Jim and my best friend Lily for all you've done, too."

With that, Marco began to move away from the podium. There was silence. It was stunning.

Then came a clap, and another, and soon he had a standing ovation. A few in the crowd could tell that this boy turned man was destined for something great in his future.

TWENTY-SIX

"Marco, we are all so proud of you." Anita smiled as she reached up to hug him.

Marco was grinning from ear to ear. As he hugged her back, he was nodding here and there as he made eye contact with his classmates. Draped in his black cap and gown, he stood on Georgetown University's Healy Lawn. The afternoon was comfortable but gray and overcast. A warm wind from the Chesapeake Bay blew across the grounds as cherry blossoms took flight. Gray skies had threatened to move the ceremony indoors to McDonough Arena, but Mother Nature had cooperated and provided the diverse and international student body an opportunity to share one more experience together.

"Pete, thanks for coming, too," Marco said as he extended his hand to Pete Matli, who'd traveled to Washington with Anita.

"Attaboy, Marco! You are a chip off the old block!" Pete said, but seeming a little on edge and uncomfortable. He was rarely together with Anita when Jim was also present. While it had been several years since their split, Jim and Anita remained friends and vested partners in their family, their children, and, at times, their respective interests. But Jim barely tolerated Pete.

Marco next turned to Jim. This embrace was different as the two men hugged each other tightly. They held their embrace for many seconds, and Jim patted Marco's back several times. It was a moving moment for both of them, and most notably, nothing was said. Nothing needed to be said.

As they broke their embrace, Jim grabbed Marco's shoulders to size him up. Marco stood an inch taller. Marco was vibrant with a big smile and radiant, intelligent, brown eyes.

"Well done. Outstanding," Jim said as he shook his head slowly.

"Keep your eye on the prize, right, Jim? Work hard and stay focused and you can…"

"Change the world," they both said together as they laughed out loud.

"Let's walk," Marco said.

"You boys go along. Peter and I need to get things together to make our flight. Marco, we really are all so proud of you," Anita said.

They parted ways, and Jim and Marco began to stroll down one of the many pathways that led through the university's campus. "I know you know this, but I want to say it again. I am grateful for all you and Anita have done for me," Marco said. They moved along the walkway next to Healy Lawn, past Lauinger Library, and farther into the center of Georgetown's impressive campus. There were families all along the pathway and near buildings, taking photographs and memorializing their own student's achievements. Here and there, Marco would see a classmate or friend and nod or wave.

"I know. Listen, I've got some things lined up for you. A good friend in Capital Markets at Klyner Peabody wants you to interview with him. And remember those guys I was talking about at Silver Lake? They'd love to speak to you as well. I really want you to fly out to San Fran and meet them. Some of these roles are going to be two- or three-year commitments only, but you can go back and get an MBA afterward. And—" Marco cut him off.

"Wait a minute. I have been thinking a lot about my future," Marco said as he raised his hand. There was a pause. "Listen, Jim, I am going home to Argentina, not to New York, San Francisco, or Texas. This past year, I was considering a bunch of options and working out what I wanted to do next. Don't get me wrong; I love the United States. But I belong in Argentina." He spoke with a tone of authority and determination.

Jim was taken by surprise. "Marco, there is so much instability there. You have such great roots here. Seriously, you have a bright future no matter what you consider doing here. I thought we spoke about you seeking your US citizenship?"

"Jim, I don't want to let you down. I really don't. God knows I appreciate all of the kindness and all of the effort you've put forth in helping me get my education. But my decision is already made. I have been accepted to Facultad de Derecho." By now they were entering Dahlgren Quad, where Marco had enjoyed many spring afternoons studying, learning, and engaging with his classmates.

"Marco, I can't let you just blow off your education!" Now Jim was becoming agitated, and while he didn't realize it, it was mostly because he was losing his own vicarious aspirations for Marco, seeing Marco's choices as ones he would be making if their roles were reversed. "You have all of the right gifts to do something great with your life. I mean it; these are some great opportunities for you. And these aren't the only ones: I have even spoken to several business associates in Houston who'd love to—"

"DAD!...I mean, Jim." The burst of frustration and the "dad" caught both of them off guard, as if a loud noise had broken their focus, and for a split second, they were in a different conversation. Marco smiled as if embarrassed; Jim smiled with adoration and affection, and in his heart felt the love a father feels when a son says, "I'm proud of you, Dad." The moment settled the tension instantly. Jim sighed, still smiling.

"I'm not following..." Jim said quietly, looking down as they began walking again and slowly shaking his head.

"I've been accepted to Facultad de Derecho. It is one of Argentina's most prestigious law schools. Like Georgetown, they have provided me a scholarship. I intend to attain my law degree and then see what I can do with it. But there, not here. And there's something more. I don't want you to continue to support me financially. I worked on this alone because I knew that if I involved you, you might feel an obligation to help me or provide some continued financial support. You have done enough for me. I have been well equipped. Remember what you used to say about scouting and having skills?"

"In life, if we have poor skills, we need a lot of gear, and if we have strong skills, we need very little gear. And this is an analogy for life, where gear is like help. Great skills require little help," Jim said, smiling with mixed emotions but also impressed with what he was hearing.

"Yep. I have been impeccably equipped, but now I must move on with what I have to do and see what I can do with what I have been given," Marco said.

"Will you get a job?" Jim asked as his mind was turning.

"I'll find something. Wait tables or something like that."

They walked for a while in silence, heading toward Marco's dormitory. They had moved farther away from the graduation ceremony, but the campus remained vibrant as students and faculty members were returning from the ceremony or moving toward activities. Marco was looking for affirmation. Jim wanted to give it, but he was still running through all kinds of questions. "Law school...well, that's pretty impressive actually," he thought.

Jim's attention turned inward. He was grieving. He longed for memories of days when his children were younger and of times they shared as young adults. There were only a few, but these were the memories that he cherished most. Comparatively he had thousands more of boardroom presentations, road shows, red-eye flights, and power lunches. He'd put so much time into his career. When Marco came into his life, he'd made changes and missed meetings and lost deals. He'd put his priorities in a better order. But now he was grieving about what might be stolen away by distance. Argentina was not a ride over the river or a day trip. He'd relished his newly organized priorities, and now Marco was leaving. Jim was grieving.

"Marco, I just don't know what to say. I guess I am surprised, but I guess you have to do what you think your life is leading you to do," Jim said.

The entire flight home was heartbreaking. Jim was near tears, but he also wanted to find a way to support Marco. While Marco was not his son, Jim had done everything but legally adopt him. Jim loved him greatly and wanted to show support, and perhaps he could also find a way to stay involved. An idea occurred to him.

When Jim got off the plane, he texted Marco. "Just landed! Call me when you get a minute."

A few hours later on the phone, Jim said, "Did you like working on the ranch with me?" Marco had spent his summers at Georgetown in Jim's employ. After Jim and Anita split, Jim sold the majority of his interest in his business. He remained as chairman and retained a minority interest. They called him occasionally to open some doors and keep warm some of his extensive relationships, but he was bought out handsomely and poured his interests into his ranch, where he was breeding cattle. He was a gentlemen rancher, but one with impeccable commercial instincts. He'd leveraged a fat wallet to build an outstanding herd of Brahman. This type of cattle was heat tolerant, and his bulls were some of the breed's grand champions. Because he ran the ranch like a business, his foreman had been recruited in the same way a private equity firm finds a management team. Together, they'd turned a big spread to a bigger breeding operation, leasing additional land and selling their bulls to other breeders who were looking to improve the quality of their own herds.

"Yeah! Sure, that place is great, and the work is awesome! But I'm not going to be a *caballero*. I am a city boy, remember, Jim."

"No, that's not what I am saying. I just have an idea. There might be a way for you to make a little extra money while you are in school." There was a long silence. "Marco, promise me you will stay in touch. I'm not getting younger, but any thanks are really from me to you. I treasure our relationship. I am proud of you. That's for sure. But I also consider you a great friend…and well, I know I ride you sometimes like a father rides a son, but I always did what I did because I love you. You were and are a very dear friend. Please promise me we'll remain in touch. The only thing I fear about your plans is never seeing or talking to you again. That's the only thing that would really hurt."

"Jim, we will always be in touch. Besides, who else am I going to call if I need to borrow some money?" At that they both started laughing.

BOOK THREE
LEGACY

TWENTY-SEVEN

It was late, and Marco was tired. He'd had a long day, and as he packed up his belongings, he replayed the day's events.

As a staff attorney for the city attorney of Buenos Aires, he'd entered the conference room early and found a chair against a wall, away from the table. It was a large, elegant, but tired, room with a single board-style table of Brazilian mahogany wrapped in black leather. Chairs for twenty sat at the table, with simpler chairs along the walls for lower-level professionals. Along the wall hung portraits of previous leaders in business suits and grins, espousing confidence. As the hour approached for the meeting, more and more members of the mayor's staff arrived. The mayor of Buenos Aires was perhaps the third-most-powerful position in Argentina. Buenos Aires was at the center of the large country—the capital, the financial hub, the industrial engine, and the main gateway, through its port, for the country. Mayors became governors, and some even made it to the highest offices of the land.

The room eventually became full, with standing room only. This was a big meeting, and everyone was under tremendous pressure. The mayor was feeling great political heat on all sides as he was trying to fulfill a campaign promise, and in doing so, not squander his legacy. But, as a typical politician, he was really focused on the next election.

The trial was just a month away. The suit aimed to vest the city with the power to force the relocation of thousands of poor families to new housing outside of the city's center. The mayor was trying to tackle all kinds of problems, ranging from cleaning up the city, to improving the crime rate, to giving some valuable land to friends and developers, to improving the tax base in what were today shantytowns of government-owned "projects." One of the shantytowns in question was Villa Thirty-One. Marco was both well informed and emotionally tied to Villa Thirty-One's fate. But he was a low-level attorney, and no one had asked his opinion. At least not until today.

As the meeting began, the fireworks almost immediately started. The mayor was adamant. "We absolutely must find a way to make this happen. I have too much riding on this. Now tell me how we pull this off...and I don't want any excuses...No is not an option."

"We can win this case. Legally, we have the right to condemn this property, and there is absolutely no legal standard or position that should disrupt a successful outcome," the lead city attorney said.

"Yeah, but you are going to get killed on this. As we get closer to the vote, the riots and protests are going to dominate the headlines, and your supporters are already backing away. Last month your approval ratings were off another ten percent, and we are now below fifty percent. The papers are hammering you, and the longer these riots go on, the more you will lose support and voters. The opposition is in your face, and they are winning both the press and the popular opinion," said the mayor's top political advisor, the man who'd been the architect of his successful run for mayor.

"Change is never easy, and we have to find a way to move forward," said the mayor.

"Sometimes you have to choose your timing...I agree, it's a priority, but it could make you a one-term mayor, and your chances at higher office will be lost. It comes down to what you are willing to sacrifice...I never thought this was a good idea," the advisor said.

It was one of those moments where children around the room got nervous as they watched mom and dad go at it. The mayor and his advisor were incredibly close, but they went toe-to-toe often. The advisor was logical and in this regard completely incapable of bringing the personal passion necessary to win over voters in an election in South America. The mayor was emotional, very animated, intense, and believable, like a furniture salesman on late-night TV. He'd won because the logic of his arguments was faultless, and the passion of his appeal was palpable. While they had these battles, they needed each other and always found the middle ground. But spectators always got uncomfortable when things became heated between them.

"You can't walk on this now, not after what you've put into it!" the attorney butted in, growing agitated.

There was a moment of silence that was broken as one person turned to another and asked a question, which led to a few other sidebars. Before one minute had passed, the room was bubbling with the noise of a number of different conversations. Marco raised his hand and sat quietly waiting for recognition. He didn't want to overstep his position, but he wasn't sure how to bring it up.

As he was conferring with someone nearby, the mayor saw the hand and paused, looking around at the breakdown and the disorder; he wanted to bring everyone back together.

He raised his head as if to invite Marco to speak. Slowly Marco lowered his hand and stood up, looking around to see whether it was OK to speak. All eyes turned to him as the room quieted.

"Remind me your name, Mario?...uh?..." the mayor said.

"Marco Segrato, sir." This caught the mayor by surprise. How had he not known a Segrato was working for him? The family had been significant donors and even hosted fundraisers for him: one in their mansion in Palermo and the other out at the estate in Mendoza where the family bottled a very popular wine. He didn't want to seem insulting and wasn't sure whose son this was, but he wasn't about to get in trouble with Señor Segrato. "Yeah, yeah, Marco...I'm sorry," he said with a charismatic furniture-salesman smile on his face.

The room was silent. Marco's boss loved him and knew he was smart, but even he was a little miffed that Marco was speaking up.

"I think there is a different way to approach this. Right now the press is billing this as an aggressive use of the city's power of eminent domain to displace poor people who couldn't rebuild even if they were given the chance. But I think there is a greater opportunity here, and you might consider approaching this a little differently." Everyone was quiet but turned their heads to the mayor, like in a tennis match. The mayor nodded and raised his hand as if to say, "OK, so what?" so Marco continued. All eyes turned back to the young attorney.

"The properties that make up these communities are worth millions, maybe even hundreds of millions. We should see them as economic revitalization zones. The people we are displacing need help. They need job skills and opportunities to improve their living conditions. And Argentina needs to continue to provide laborers to heavy industry, which is virtuous because the more companies that can expand, the more jobs we can create, which creates growth for the economy. Because these people may not be the most skilled, we should tie their relocation to the opportunity for job skills. If we recast the plans for relocation and invest in affordable housing where job skills can be provided in learning centers and where new industry can tap into these newly trained workers, perhaps you'd turn what appears to be a negative into a positive."

"How are we going to pay for that? It's pie in the sky," someone said.

"Not really," Marco said calmly as he turned to address the heckler. "We impose a special tax on developers of new property in the economic revitalization zones, and we issue bonds against this tax revenue to pay for the investment in the new communities. We provide industry tax credits for companies who hire people from these programs and have the companies partner with us to develop the skills-based training programs. If Grupo Tampico needs five hundred more employees for their new plant, we share the cost of the training and provide them tax relief for every new employee who comes through the training program and sticks with them for more than a year. This gives them incentive to train and hire these people. It gives the displaced families a chance to start fresh, hopefully with new skills and good jobs. It gives the developers what they want, the land to build on, and it allows us to finance the transition. And we look like we are helping poor families make better lives by giving them a way out of the ghettos and toward employment."

There was silence as people contemplated it. The advisor was first to speak. "I can see how we can reposition and reframe what you want to do, Mr. Mayor. I like the idea that those who might profit from this, the developers, will be paying for it through higher taxes. And I think it changes the argument the opposition has because they don't have any other solutions for the poor people besides give them their right to stay put. I like it."

"The developers will balk; there's no way—" someone said before getting interrupted.

"*The developers!* They will fall in line. You say hundreds of millions; I say potentially billions are at stake for them. Each one of these communities, if turned over to them for office, residential, and commercial use, will become a gold mine in time. Hell, prices are already being driven up as more and more people want to move into town. The developers will be with us," the mayor said.

The meeting turned to tackling this idea, and orders and instructions were being handed out among the most-senior members of the staff. Slowly, members of the meeting left to get back to work, and eventually the mayor himself left. The few remaining, including Marco, gathered their things and walked out. On his way out, a colleague caught Marco's attention. "Good job today… That was impressive."

"Let's see whether it has legs first," Marco said. "It feels good to contribute," he thought.

He returned to his desk to get back to work. He listened to his voice mail first. "Hi, baby! I hope you can come with me this weekend. There is a polo match that I want to take you to, and I know Momma will be happy to have you. Call me later, bye!"

Marco laughed. "Yeah, Momma might be OK, but your dad hates me. Not from the right side of the tracks, unfortunately," Marco thought. Marco's girlfriend, Monica Roemmers, was the beautiful scion of a wealthy family. She worked in retail and had met Marco when he was studying at a Starbucks while he attended law school. Their connection was physical and intense. But in the past few months, Monica had been increasingly trying to bring Marco to see her parents. Perhaps she was hoping for more commitment, but she was also five years younger than Marco, far less mature, and unable to really appreciate just how poor Marco was. He never made promises he couldn't keep, and he made no show of having more than he had. He was well paid now and lived in a comfortable neighborhood full of young single professionals, but he often tried to tell her that she was out of his league.

Marco next focused on e-mails. The morning was shot, but he needed to get caught up before he began looking at the legal work on his desk. Slowly but surely he was making his way through the list. Some were important and required a carefully worded response; others were just information, and some were institutionally distributed junk mail. All larger organizations had this way of cluttering inboxes and sapping productivity from their employees with totally unimportant e-mail. The City of Buenos Aires was no different.

Marco's phone rang. "Bueno," he said.

The senior advisor was on the phone. Marco had very little access to the mayor and worked a few layers down from the city attorney, but he had visited some of the political staff, including the advisor, on occasion. Along the way, the advisor had learned a little about Marco's time in the States and his degree in political science, which impressed him both because it was unique and because it was the kind of elite pedigree to be expected from donors, not from staff attorneys. "Marco, that was really good work in there. I think we can do something with your idea."

"OK, great!" Marco said and waited. There was silence.

"Can I do something for you?" Marco asked.

"Marco, the mayor wants you reassigned. Well, I guess he wants you to consider coming to work for him in his campaign office. I think it might be a good idea, and I can use some free thinkers. He likes your background and your time in Washington, DC, and of course, he thinks, and I kind of agree, the role you have there might not be the best use of your talents."

"Uhh, I, uhhh...Have you spoken to..."

"Yes, everyone here is on board, so there are no hard feelings with the city attorney if that is what you are worried about. And we can pay you well, too. We need a man to take the lead on things that relate to the mayor's next campaign, but that must happen outside of city offices."

"I am interested in it, but I have a lot of things that I am working on right now." This was catching Marco off guard.

"Marco, I want to give you some advice, just honest advice from a guy who's been around the block a bit. The things you are working on are important, I would suppose. But there is a whole different future out there. What you are working on is implementing and addressing policies. We are inviting you to work on forming, authoring, and establishing policies. There's a difference. And trust me...I know because there was a time when I was in a seat like yours and I received a call like this. These are doors that open very rarely. You can have an impact, and our mayor is going somewhere...somewhere big. Don't let this door close. You can always get a job like you have, especially with your connections and your pedigree."

Marco sat there for a minute and wondered what the advisor meant by connections. But Marco did have an excellent pedigree—high school at Colegio del Salvador, college in the United States at Georgetown University, and his law degree here in his hometown at Facultad de Derecho.

And he always had liked politics and wanted to be a part of it, to see it happen and perhaps to influence the outcomes.

"Sir, I am honored and also very interested. May I have a few days to think it over?"

"Yeah, sure, a few days. But do yourself a favor: make them think you are jumping at the chance. Remember, our boss has an ego." They both laughed.

Marco worked on some of the projects on his desk for the rest of the day but made little progress. His mind was on the offer and what he should do with it. His heart was racing with excitement and anxiety given the stability of his current role. As the sun was setting, he readied to leave the office.

TWENTY-EIGHT

Bags packed, he made his way out of the offices to the street. He was departing the Palace of the Chief of Government of Buenos Aires, which stood across from Plaza de Mayo and was at the end of Avenida de Mayo. The building was originally built in 1890 in a French architectural style that remained impressive. As he walked, he reflected on the case and what he believed about it. He was heading toward the plaza and on his way home.

Marco had graduated the year after he achieved his Eagle Scout in Houston. He and Jim had reconciled, and Marco had come to appreciate that while he was from a different background, he did indeed have some very close friends. He was embarrassed in the months that followed the service project, after he'd returned home, that he'd been so bitter toward Jim and Anita. They loved him like one of their own. They also respected his independence. He'd come to understand that Jim and Anita were trying to let Marco make his own life plans. They did not expect that Marco would decide to do things near them or that they would even see him. But Jim was always leading and directing Marco, and it was true that after he and Anita broke up, Jim had become even more connected with Marco, as a father is with his son. It had been hard for Jim when he learned of Marco's plans to return to Argentina.

What Marco knew now, but had not appreciated at seventeen, was that if someone truly loves another and the time comes, he or she will let that person go, even if it hurts. The Swansons were willing to accept that at some point Marco Segrato might decide to abandon his relationship with them. If that was a decision he made, they would be content to know they had invested in the boy's life, helped direct and resource his education, and in doing so, given him opportunities to make plans that might include them or might not.

Marco's thoughts drifted back to college. With Jim's guidance, help from his high school counselors at Colegio del Salvador, and a little help from God, he'd been accepted to Georgetown in Washington. This cool night reminded him of the autumns in Washington—brisk but not too cold. Buenos Aires rarely got very cold. DC on the other hand could be blanketed in snow. Those days were some of his favorite memories. Like many college kids, he'd dated. He remembered nights when he and his girlfriend at the time would know they'd be snowed in, and as young lovers do, they'd snuggled up with nothing on but the radio. On one such night, he'd walked three miles, partly through snow six inches deep. Despite the snow, he'd been warm enough because of the work of getting across town. But his girlfriend had come to the door with a hot chocolate to greet him, and she'd had some champagne waiting on ice to sip on while they made small talk on their way to bed.

Political science students at Georgetown were challenged by three facts. First, they were students in what was once the most important political center in the world. The United States had been the richest and most powerful nation in the world. Today DC shared that role with other capitals such as Beijing and Brussels. Second, there were few places that equaled Georgetown in the study of democracy and the strengths of the US Constitution. It didn't hurt that many of the country's preeminent constitutional lawyers were often invited to speak, teach, or lecture to students, and Marco was often in attendance while he was in school there. And third, the Jesuits' approach to education had challenged him in ways that many institutions would not have, forcing him to think, and in his thinking, draw conclusions. The Jesuits were funny: there were no right answers, just the answers driven by the students' consciences in reflection of their own values and in deference to their subjection to God, their creator.

His time at Georgetown had led him to a simple conclusion: America's prosperity, which continued although it was not as pronounced as it was around the time of Ronald Reagan or Bill Clinton, was based on a society that possessed both a skilled work force and free markets that were subjected to the rule of law and protected by individual freedoms. Marco believed passionately that any great society must copy these things to be competitive. He knew from his education that Argentina had modeled its own constitution after that of the United States. But he also believed that the country had failed to place the rule of law at the highest levels, allowing juntas and politically popular leaders like Peron and Kirchner to soften legal protections and letting corruption undermine Argentina's potential.

Having on rare occasions gone back to Villa Thirty-One to try and find his aunt and cousins, he'd also concluded that the people there would never be able to escape that environment unless they were trained with skills that could provide them trades or reliable jobs. His mother had been stuck at the bottom of the rung with no way out but prostitution and, after he was born, cleaning office buildings. If someone had taught her a skill, perhaps she would have been able to move forward. Without a skill, she was stuck. He always pictured in his mind the famous photo of Rosie the Riveter from World War II, when women had built essential items like engines and aircraft to fuel the United States' war effort. They'd been taught how to do a skilled job and many, after the war, had continued in the workforce, aiding in America's economic prosperity.

As he made his way down the street, he could hear the hum of a crowd ahead. It wasn't until he turned the corner that he remembered. "Oh crap," he thought. The people were protesting in the Plaza de Mayo, and he needed to make his way past the demonstrations to get to his home. He could tell it was raucous. He recalled from his brief scan of the papers yesterday morning that the crowd, which had been encamped for over a month now and continued to grow daily, was planning to make a statement this afternoon. It seemed, as he approached the park, that they had succeeded. He could see the police in full form standing in a perimeter around the park. The crowd was swelling and moving; it alarmed him. But since he was walking across the street from the park, he thought he'd easily be able to get through the crowd.

This was a young crowd, full of school dropouts and drug abusers, but there were other people involved, too. The elite believed the mob was protesting economic inequality and resented the fact that these protesters attacked the affluent community's success. Marco perceived the message of the crowd to be more about opportunity. He could see how they felt slighted and shortchanged. There were so many challenges to getting ahead in Argentina. He knew he was lucky, and thus he was more sympathetic to their cause. He also knew that the only way to get ahead was to work hard and make something of your situation. He believed there were no free lunches.

He walked toward the park, not through it but along the perimeter where the police were mostly located. As he approached an intersection adjacent to the park, he looked down the street and saw a huge contingent of police in riot gear. They were standing in formation but did not seem ready to pounce. He assumed they'd been brought in as a precaution—an assumption that in a few minutes proved to be a mistake.

Continuing down the block, he seemed to sense a rise in the tension from the protesters. In fact, with a few more steps, he worried that it was quickly becoming a riot. At first he thought he should just move quickly past them, but a few more steps brought the thought to turn around and take the long way home. He turned and began to hurry back toward the intersection with the riot police. As his pace quickened away from the protest, now he faced an equally disturbing threat. Around the corner in full stride came the police riot brigade. They initially turned onto his side of the street, which startled him. So instead of getting trampled or being in their way, he began to jog across to the other side of the street where the park and protest were, but he was still down the block from the crowd.

In an instant, it seemed the riot police were converging from every corner. As they hit the park, the crowd went crazy. Like cockroaches when the lights are turned on, everyone was scattering. Someone came running by him at full speed, knocking his briefcase out of his hands and pushing him hard. He went to grab the case, but two or three more rioters blew by, pushing him off balance. A moment later, he had his briefcase under his arm. Looking back, he saw only mayhem behind him. He realized he needed to start running, too.

As he did, he was caught by an even larger crew of protesters running at full speed out of fear and rage. Next to him, a projectile landed. He immediately realized the police were now firing tear gas. Things were in total chaos. The police, who had been clamping down across the street, were now moving into the crowd on his side of the street. With full gear, including batons, they broke into crews to attack individual demonstrators. Marco needed to get out of this place as quickly as possible.

People were no longer running in his direction or passing him. People were moving in any and every direction. He had his eyes fixed on finding a path back to his office, where he hoped to be out of harm's way, not watching the spectacle or those around him. As he zigzagged to miss people, he kept his line toward his office. He was now passing rioters and riot police; some of them were engaged in physical altercations.

Suddenly he was hit hard across the back and then again on the shoulder, throwing him down to a knee. Marco was a big guy, so taking him down was difficult. He wasn't sure what had happened. He just tried to get up and get away, but this time he was hit several times, which pushed him back to the ground. In the midst of pain, with a shocked sense of losing control, he realized he'd been mistaken for a protester. The police were on him with a small crew. He went limp, trying to show he meant no harm, but they showed no mercy.

"I am not one of them! *Stop! I am a lawyer!*" The beating continued for a few more seconds, but he lay on the ground in a submissive manner, and the police had other problems. Now members of the mob were on this group of cops. The police crew quickly became outnumbered. The balance of power had shifted, and now the police were overwhelmed. As the protesters attacked the police, a woman grabbed Marco. "Get up! Let's get out of here...hurry!" she said.

Marco found his footing. With her help, he got up to run with her. He was hurt, limping and acting only from instinct to survive and escape. They ran together, running for their lives away from the park and the police.

TWENTY-NINE

The girl was slowing enough to look over at him. "Did they hurt you?" she asked in their native Spanish. Both were breathing deeply, and neither had registered much about the other. Now she could see he was tall and seemed a little older than she was. He looked a little ashen. "Are you hurt?" she asked again.

"I dunno…" His answer was quiet, and he slowed down to a walk, drawing deep breaths. He was hurting but wasn't sure where. He was also thinking about his briefcase. It had taken on a strange sense of importance in the chaos. It would probably seem silly later, but his mind stayed focused on it nevertheless. The last thing he could recall was being pounded to the ground by several officers, and then someone kicking the briefcase away, perhaps because they thought it could be used as a weapon.

"Oh my God, you're bleeding!" She was startled as she reached up to his shoulder and pushed him to a stop, causing him to turn toward her.

"Where?" Marco asked, looking down his front, trying to see blood. Seeing none, he was raising his hand to his head when she reached behind his right triceps and gently pulled his arm forward, trying to reveal his elbow. The right arm of his dress shirt was covered in blood from the elbow to his shirt cuff. "Funny, I don't hurt there; it's just a scratch." He didn't smile, and it wasn't really funny. Marco looked out of sorts, his mind unfocused, as if he were in shock.

"Where should we go?" she asked. She stood about five foot four and had a crazy haircut like a punk rocker from the eighties or Bellatrix from the Harry Potter movies. She wasn't as dark as that character, but her hair spiked at the top. On one side the hair had a buzz cut, and on the other it was long but stuck tight to her head. It was jet black at the scalp and bleached blond at the tips of her spike. Her makeup was thick, and her eye shadow was a heavy, deep blue. Her lipstick was black. She also wore a nose ring and several earrings. Marco had seen girls like her before in the barrios.

"I gotta go home. I think I am hurt, and I need to lie down," he said.

"Where do you live?" She began to look around to try and figure out where she should go. She didn't need trouble with the law and was making certain they had not been followed.

"Just down here; I can make it. Do you know where you are? Can you get home from here?" Marco was not very attentive to her body language. His mind was a little foggy, and he hurt all over. He was thinking of getting home and not about where she might need to go.

"Uhh...yeah, I know where we are, but...I'll walk you home. You look pretty beat up, and you might need a little help," she said.

"No, I'm cool. You don't need to...but I gotta go. You sure you know your way home from here?" Marco was now looking at her; he needed to make sure he wasn't leaving her stranded.

"Let me walk you up the block, and then I'll let you go," she said.

They made their way down the street to the next block where Marco lived. As he had approached the park earlier when the mayhem had broken out, he'd turned around and then bolted across the street, away from his home. But after he was accosted by the police and beaten to the ground, he must have gotten spun around. When the woman had grabbed him and they'd broken out in their frenzied run, he hadn't had an aim; he had just run with her through the crowd, turning and turning to ensure he didn't get in front of another group of riot police. He'd actually run across the park and back to the side he was intending to get to in the first place, nearer his home. As they had run past the park and down several more blocks, they'd come close to his apartment building.

It was a nice building—not fancy, but certainly upper end, especially for the girl. "This is my stop. Listen, thanks for picking me up and helping me get out of there. I don't really know what happened, but I am glad you grabbed me when you did. Are you sure you know your way home?" he said as they approached the building. His eyes were locked on hers, and he could tell she was uncertain. "Do you have a place to go now?" he asked because he knew some of the rioters had been living in tents and hanging out at the park during their protest. It had been peaceful until tonight, and he started thinking she might have been with the crowd. She looked like she could be one of those people.

She was looking both ways and looking nowhere. She was thinking, and he started worrying she might not have a good answer. "Listen, why don't you come up to my place and have some water or tea. We can calm down a bit, and you can help me clean my arm up."

"OK!" She brightened. She had nowhere else to go.

They made their way into his flat. It was comfortable. He'd made some good money while at Georgetown and had continued to enjoy a decent income while in law school. He was twenty-six years old now and had a pretty cool flat. She was definitely impressed. As he turned on the lights and they made their way into the flat, he saw her for the first time. She was pretty rough. Her hair was out of control, and while she was pretty, she looked tired and haggard. "She probably does a lot of drugs," he thought. If she worked, she probably didn't make much money because her clothes were cheap—she was dressed like a tramp. He guessed she was a few years younger than he was. He was also a little suspicious seeing her in the light and thought he'd have to watch his stuff. Her manner didn't seem suspicious, but she looked it the way she was dressed.

"Listen, I need to get these clothes off. We've both been through a lot, and I know I am tired. I bet you are, too. Would you like to use the restroom or clean up a little bit? Can I get you some tea or a soda?" he asked.

She nodded yes, and he led her to the guest bathroom. It was off of the living area, adjacent to the kitchen, and connected to the second bedroom. She locked the doors, and as he returned to the kitchen to get her a soda, he heard the shower start. "Hmm… make yourself at home," he thought.

While she showered, Marco got his shirt off and threw it away. He was using a cloth on his arm, still wearing an undershirt. He was more worried about his back and his side. They had been hit hard. While there was a pretty bad gash on his elbow from the fall, the hits were what hurt him the most.

A few minutes later, she came out looking very different. Her hair was down, and the makeup was off. She had freckles and a nice complexion, but she had bags under her eyes. For a young woman, she seemed as if she'd lived a difficult and perhaps rough life. She looked as if she'd already been worn down some.

"I take it you don't have a home to go to, right?" Marco asked with genuine sympathy as they sat down at his breakfast table.

She looked down and shook her head slowly no. She felt shame. "So, why were you out there? What are you fighting for?" she asked Marco. She wanted to change the subject, deflect him from talking about her.

He laughed out loud, which confused her. "I wasn't out there!" he said as he opened his hands while shaking his head back in forth. "I was just walking home from work and then all hell broke loose; the next thing I knew some cops were pounding me, I lost my briefcase, and you came flying through the crowd, picked me up, and told me to run as fast as I could!" he said, unable to believe what had happened.

"From work? You weren't part of the movement? Well, I guess that makes sense. Living in a place like this, you must have work. What do you do?" She wanted to keep the focus on him and away from herself, but she asked it with a sincere interest. Her body perked up as she asked.

"I am a lawyer for the City of Buenos Aires," he said proudly, all smiles.

"Ahh, a lawyer. That sounds important. Is it a good job?" She'd known some lawyers. She'd known some doctors, too. Doctors, lawyers, bankers—they were all the same to her.

"I guess it's a good job. What do you do?"

She turned away quickly, as if the question cut her. "I don't work. I just hang with my friends." She was masking something, and he could tell. He was no expert trial lawyer, but he'd already deposed enough people in his short career that he could tell when someone was beating around the bush.

"Seriously, you have to have a way to make a living." As he said this, the light went off. The clothing, the hair, the earrings, and no home—it all came together. "Where did you grow up? I was born in Villa Thirty-One; ever heard of it?"

She was floored and looked at him in disbelief. "No way," she thought. Slowly her eyes left him, and she looked down at the ground. "I am from there, but I don't live there anymore. Listen, you don't want to know about me. I am not worth knowing about." Her voice trailed off. She continued to look down, and as she did, he felt tremendous compassion. He was certain now: she was a prostitute, making her living on the streets turning tricks. As he looked at her, and she looked at the ground, his mind went back to his mother. This woman was his mother, just thirty years later. The longer she worked her trade, the more likely it was that she'd have her own child or children and repeat the cycle his mother had so desperately wanted to end.

She was restless, so she stood up and began walking around the flat. As she did, her eyes were drawn to the photos. "There is no way this guy is from the barrio," she thought. She was also deeply ashamed to speak about herself or to open up.

He was watching her and figured she was trying to check it all out, but he was also cautious. Something inside told him to trust her.

"Is this you in the uniform? Were you in some military school?" she asked.

"No, I am an Eagle Scout. It was a program I was involved in as a child in the United States called the Boy Scouts of America. It helps prepare young boys for adulthood through all kinds of cool activities." He smiled.

"So you aren't from the barrio, are you?" She was perturbed.

"Not true!" He was smiling even more now because he knew she was digging, and he was going to one-up her, but in a sporting way, not condescending or competitive. "See the photo over there, on the side table? It is an old photo and not in good shape. It is my mother. She was a prostitute in the barrio, in Villa Thirty-One, when I was born. She turned her life around and through faith and hard work raised me as best she could." Now his voice grew more somber as he touched the nerve in his own heart about her and how she died. It was his turn to hold things close. "She died unexpectedly, and I was adopted by some Americans who helped me with my education. That's them over there. Their names are Jim and Anita. They helped me make it through high school and college, and I even worked for Jim here in Buenos Aires, sort of."

She continued around the room. "You like cows?" she said with a laugh.

"Yeah. I love beef, too!" He laughed back. With that, she turned and met his eyes. Hers were coy and curious, and her face said, "Well?"

"When I graduated from high school, I went to school in the United States. Then I came here to attend law school. Jim, the man who adopted me, was a really successful businessman who retired and bought a ranch in Arkansas. Ever heard of Arkansas?" She shook her head no. "Well, it is one of the fifty United States and is really beautiful country. Because he was worried about me having enough money for law school, he paid me to travel all around Argentina and call on estancias selling...well, this sounds weird, but believe me, it's true...selling bull semen!"

She gasped loudly and laughed at the same time. He was chuckling quietly because he knew it was just so preposterous—some kid traveling across the backcountry selling sperm from cows. As they were both relishing the humor in it, he continued. "Well, honestly, I know it sounds strange, but I spent my weekends promoting these champion bulls while Jim's ranch hands were pulling what are called 'straws' from those bulls to sell here. One of the big things we did was show the quality of the bulls and the quality of the cows. A top bull will sell a straw, which is used to inseminate cows to improve an estancia's herd, for fifty to a hundred dollars. I met a bunch of cool people, mostly wealthy ranchers, throughout the country. And I made a little money, too. What was funniest is how I'd get access. They all thought I was some rich guy's son or nephew because of my name…Hey! I don't even know your name!"

"I don't know your name, either…So what is it?"

"No way, you go first. I made the tea!" Again he was sporting with her, but in a fun way. She took the lead and played along, also enjoying the fun.

"OK, I'll go first, but only one of my names. Then you tell me one of yours. My first name is Catalina. Now what is your first name?"

"Fair enough; my first name is Marco. What is your second name?"

"I don't have a second name; I just have a last name." She stuck her lower lip out as if to pout. "It's Valdez."

"Well, I can't top that. I don't have a middle name, either. My second and last name is Segrato."

Her eyes got wide, and her eyebrows rose. The Segrato name was well known because of the popular wine, and she thought they were super-rich and famous, too.

"It's not what you think. The guy from the picture, Jim, knew a famous businessman named Jose Carlo Segrato. He died a few years ago, but anyway, when my mom died—and trust me, it's a long story—Jim needed a way to help with my education legally. And so, somehow, money was set aside for me. Well, because I was from the barrio, and no one was really sure of my last name and didn't bother to ask me, they effectively changed my name without asking…I was ten years old and…" Catalina's face turned sad with empathy. Children in the barrios often had difficult stories to tell from their childhoods. Hers was one of sexual abuse. "Well, I was pretty confused about what was happening. Nevertheless, all of the grownups agreed that my name would be Marco Segrato, and they said it would ensure I would be well provided for. The funny thing is, I've never met Mr. Segrato…in fact, I've never met any of the Segratos!"

"It's a pretty well-known name. And they make a good wine!" Catalina said as if to look on the bright side.

"Exactly! That is exactly right! Look at this." Marco got up, and they went to his bedroom, where he showed her a lamp on his dresser. It was a bottle of one of the Segratos' Malbecs turned into a lamp. "My friends gave this to me when I graduated law school." He sat there, looking at the bottle and reminiscing. As they looked at the bottle, she slowly turned to look at him. She trusted him now. His smile was fading though, and she asked him what was wrong.

"I am really hurting. I probably need to lie down and go to sleep. Do you mind?"

She walked to the living room, and he followed her as if to close the door but saw her pick up some of her belongings. "No! No! I don't mean you have to leave…I am not thinking all that clearly. Can you just stay in the guest room and let me get some sleep? Honestly, you are welcome here, but those guys beat me up pretty good, and I think I need to lie down."

She smiled widely. "Yes, yes, of course! I will just be in the guest room." As they went to different rooms, she looked back as his door closed. She made a decision to check on him every hour or so. As he hit the bed, he was immediately asleep.

THIRTY

Catalina checked on Marco several times through the night, quietly walking across from her guest bedroom to his, opening his door, and listening carefully for his breathing. Once or twice, she made her way to his bedside to ensure he was sleeping soundly and safely. Shortly after midnight, she stood beside his bed looking down on him, wondering about and reflecting on his story of escaping the barrio. She longed to be out, too. As she stood by him, she felt a sense of déjà vu. There was something familiar about him, but she couldn't place it. She tried to stay awake, but the night eventually caught up with her.

After three or four in the morning, she fell into a deep sleep. Across the way, Marco's deep recuperating sleep was wearing off, and he was becoming fitful in the same predawn hours. He rolled over at one point and was jolted by a sharp pain from the beating he'd taken. But eventually, he dozed back off, drifting in and out until he recalled Catalina. The thrill of meeting her captured his consciousness, and again his slumber was lost. After a while he dozed again, until his sleep was again disrupted, this time, by some excitement regarding the new job offer. The mix of it all—the pain from his encounter with police, his butterflies about meeting Catalina, and the opportunity for a new job with the campaign— were all he could take. By six, he was showered and working. His first order of business was to leave a message calling in sick. He next reached out to an office friend via text, sharing what had happened in more detail. "OMG! UNBELIEVABLE!" his friend responded. Marco called his boss's cell phone to inform him of his absence and also to share more details of the police encounter so his boss understood why he'd be missing work. Eventually, he called the mayor's political advisor.

"I wanted to reach out to you and follow up on your offer. I know this is a big opportunity for me, and I want to do it." Marco's voice was quiet and labored.

"OK, that's great. Why don't we meet over at my office in an hour," the advisor said.

"Well, this is why I called you first thing, so early. I am not going to make it down to the office today, and I might be out for a few days. I got roughed up a little bit last night, and I need to make sure nothing is broken."

"What? What happened?" The advisor was alarmed and wasn't sure how to respond.

"You're not going to believe this, but I was at my office late last night. When I left, well, I live on the other side of Plaza de Mayo Park and..."

"Where the demonstrators were protesting? The news is all over last night's riot. It's a political disaster; what happened to you?"

"Oh, I hadn't even checked on that...makes sense. Well, this is a little crazy, but I was trying to get past the park at precisely the wrong time. As I was trying to get around the protesters, the riot police descended, and all hell broke loose. I mean, there were people scattering everywhere, and I got shoved as things escalated. Next thing I knew, I was on the ground and some police were beating on me as if I were one of the rioters. I kept yelling that I was just passing through, but it was total chaos. What is the news reporting?"

"Your voice sounds labored; are you badly hurt? You need to see a doctor. There's video of the chaos. Between the riot gear and the tear gas and the crowd going every direction, it looks like it was a real shit show. We need to start building on those ideas you had, and we need you here. But if you are hurt, you need to take care of that first. Why don't you go see a doctor? Take my cell phone number, and let's stay in touch via text. Let me know when you can be back here. These circus events are often part of the job, and we don't need you to manage the damage control. I want you looking at the big picture and thinking strategically about the campaign, so just get well. Maybe you can start with us in the next week or two; that will give you a chance to wrap up your open items and hand off any duties you need to let go. Sound good?"

"Yeah, that's perfect. Listen, I am really excited about this. I may not sound like it because my shoulder, arm, and torso are all hurting really badly"—Marco laughed—"but I'll be there in top shape as soon as possible. Thanks again!"

While he was speaking to the mayor's advisor, Catalina heard his voice from across the small flat.

She got out of bed and walked over to his bedroom, where he was on the phone and speaking quietly. When he hung up, she tapped on the door.

"How are you feeling, Marco Segrato?"

She startled him, but he turned around with a big smile that turned quickly to a moan. "Ouch! Uhhh, well, I am doing great except that I feel as if someone dropped a load of rocks on me last night. How did you sleep, Catalina Valdez?" he asked.

"Very nicely, thank you. Do you have to go to work now?"

"No, lawyers are allowed to call in sick when they are recovering from police beatings." They both laughed.

"Do you need to go? I mean, you can stay here…No, that is not what I mean. I mean: I'd like you to stay, if you can."

She smiled and nodded that she would like to stay. "I need to shower. OK?"

"How about I make us some coffee and breakfast, and you shower? Do you need anything?"

"I only have one set of clothes," she said.

"Why don't you let me give you my robe, and I'll wash your clothes? There is a quick cycle, and I can have everything done in about an hour. While you shower, I'll make us coffee and breakfast, and then we can visit while your clothes are finishing. How does that sound?"

"I like the sound of that." She walked away to the other bathroom. Marco slowly got up and went to his closet and pulled out a clean robe to give her. As he made his way to the other side of the flat, he could hear the water running. He gently knocked on the bathroom door, and she said, "Don't peek!" as she cracked the door open and handed him her clothes while grabbing the robe. Marco was looking away as she glanced through the door to see him. She smiled. "Thank you," she said.

Marco went about getting the clothes going in the washing machine and making some toast and coffee. He pulled some fresh jam, butter, and eggs from the refrigerator. He liked a soft-boiled egg in the morning, so he plopped two eggs into a pot of cold water and added a timer Anita had given him one Christmas to help cook the eggs precisely. He turned the stove on to heat the pot.

The coffee's brew cycle was up, and he realized he had no cream or milk. He liked his coffee black, and suddenly he worried he'd be a bad host. He got his sugar out of the cabinet, poured some into a bowl, pulled a small spoon out of the drawer, and placed everything on the kitchen table. He assessed what else he should have out, quickly grabbing two small plates, two butter knives, a spoon for the jam, and napkins. He so often ate on the run that he rarely prepared a table for a date. The best he could do was to remember the grand holiday dinners and parties that Anita had hosted. His table was not as fancy, but her template gave him a respectable idea of what he should do.

As the washing machine beeped, indicating the end of a quick wash cycle, Catalina was coming out of the bathroom. Her hair was wet. "Marco, do you have a hair dryer?"

"Uhh, yeah, I think so. But I am not sure how good it is...Give me a minute." He noticed her freckles and how sweet her complexion was without the makeup. It captivated him for a minute as their eyes locked on one another. Smiles were exchanged, and then he went to see what he could offer her. Returning a moment later, he had an old hair dryer.

"I'll just be a minute, OK?" she asked.

"Sure."

"I am looking forward to breakfast with you!" she said, looking at the table, impressed.

He moved her clothes over to the dryer on a gentle setting, inspecting the fabric and contemplating how long each item should dry. He blushed as he handled her undergarments.

Next he checked on the eggs and poured coffee for both of them. A few minutes later, she emerged, looking quite different from the night before. While the haircut was the same, it fell naturally, without the spikes. He liked her natural state better. As she approached the kitchen, he asked her whether she'd like to sit while he set everything on the table. In a second or two, and a few short trips, he had it all set up just as he'd planned.

She stood next to her chair, waiting for him to finish and watching the effort he showed to prepare the simple breakfast. As he was about to sit down, she reached over and grabbed his hand. "Thank you. This is very nice," she said quietly. She pulled his hand closer to herself, and in doing so, she pulled him closer as well. In one motion, she led his arm around her back and reached up to kiss him. They embraced for a second, and then their eyes met. He became the aggressor and kissed her back for longer this time as he wrapped his arms around her and pulled her close. Slowly they engaged in a long embrace, which piqued both of their senses. She reached her hands up to his chest and sought to take his shirt off, which was just fine with him. By now the robe had fallen open, exposing her bare body as flesh met flesh.

The dryer hummed on, and the food cooled on the table. For the next several hours, they made love delicately, careful not to hurt any part of Marco's aching body. There was nothing erotic or visceral about it; instead they engaged in the soft, passionate, and intimate manner of two lovers falling for each other, with little needing to be said.

As morning moved to afternoon, and after a few naps following their encounters, they both noticed they were starving. Catalina spoke up first. "Marco, I think I need to eat, but I don't want to end this." She was beaming.

"I was hoping you would say something about being hungry! I bet your clothes are finished drying now. I think it's been about five hours." They both laughed.

There were no inhibitions. He got up and walked over to the laundry. As he was grabbing clothes out, she rubbed up against him, surprising him from behind. "Thank you," she said with a hug and a kiss.

"You are welcome. Here are these; do you think we need to iron them?"

"No, you go get dressed, and I'll get myself ready, too. Let's go get something to eat," she said.

THIRTY-ONE

The rest of their day was splendid. Marco took her to a nice, local café he enjoyed. They talked about the evening before while reading the newspaper's reports. After lunch, they took a stroll back to the park to see what was happening. As with big cities, the evidence of the events was long gone. Most of the movement's demonstrators had packed up and fled. The city had a large force of officers on guard, and weekday workers were making their way here and there.

Walking hand-in-hand, they found a bench under a tree near where they thought they had first met. Catalina was sharing some of her experiences and also stories about some of the people she had met during the week-long demonstration. Most of them were out of work, hoping to make better lives for themselves but just unable. It was hard, and she shared that she was in the same boat.

"I remember my mom working two jobs. She desperately wanted a better life for herself and Mijo...that's what she called me, Mijo. I also know she had been a prostitute before I was conceived. The thought of having a baby and raising me drove her to change her course. She worked cleaning buildings, and she was active in a church. That's where I learned to read. She'd bring me to the church on Saturdays while she cleaned. The priest there,

Father Diaz, helped educate me and cared for me immediately following her death," Marco said.

"It sounds like she was very brave and very strong, Marco. It is very hard to change directions. I have tried, and sometimes I am afraid of what my boss will do if I don't work for him," Catalina said.

"Catalina, you can do anything you set your mind to. I am sure it is hard to get out of a desperate situation, but maybe you just need a little help. Like I got help from Father Diaz and the Swansons. I would be willing to help you. Would you let me?" Marco said while looking into her eyes.

Catalina turned away, looking down at the ground. As she did, she squeezed his hand, and a tear fell down her cheek. They sat in silence for a long while. Never responding, she eventually squeezed his hand twice and started to stand up. He followed her lead. Together, they began walking back to Marco's apartment.

As they strolled, Marco thought of his mother.

Marco broke the silence. "My mom and I worked one night cleaning a building. A very nice man, I've never known who he was, had given my mother a tip. That night, after she cleaned his company's offices, we left the building. As we did, we exited at the back so we could throw bags of trash away. We entered a dark alley, and two muggers attacked us. It happened very fast, but in the midst of the assault, my mom was thrown hard against the ground or a wall or something. I don't know what happened, but she hit her head, and by the next day, she had died."

Catalina was grief-stricken hearing the story. She stopped walking and turned to Marco. As he looked down at her, he saw her crying. They embraced, and she buried her face in his chest. At that moment, Marco was overcome by emotion. There was a kindred connection Marco had never felt with anyone, except perhaps with Maria, Jim and Anita's housekeeper. But she had been more like an aunt. The excitement of meeting Catalina and sharing these stories for the first time in his life since his mother's death made him feel at home. They were forming a deep connection because of their similar origins.

Eventually, they made their way back to the apartment, stopping to get takeout for dinner. It was evening, and Marco offered to open a bottle of wine. He lit a candle at the small kitchen table.

"What!" she asked, struck by the way he was staring at her.

He wanted to get her perspective on something. He also wanted to know what someone like his mother might think of his work, of the protester's movement, and of his ideas about how to get out of the barrio. "Let me ask you a question. Why don't you find a real job, a day job?"

"I've tried. There's nothing for me. I don't know how to do anything. No one will hire people like me," she said slowly, looking up as she answered.

"I am working on something that I believe in. It's a complicated plan, but there's something I'd like to know—that is, if you feel comfortable answering my questions. It relates to my project. It's just one question, but it's an important one. If I could...you know, teach you how to do a job, you know, a skill...say maybe we'd teach you to be a nurse or a healthcare technician, or maybe we'd teach you how to do a trade like plumbing or electrical work, or maybe we could teach you how to assemble something in a factory. But just think of learning a skill that would get you a good job, one you could build a career in...my question is: given where you are now, what would you give for that opportunity?"

It took her only a second to know the answer, but she was silent a long time. She was looking into his eyes and trying to read meaning into the question. There was something important about this moment, she could tell, and she could see passion in his eyes behind the question.

She began to answer quietly but emphatically. "I'd give up everything for that opportunity. I'd do it, and everyone I know would, too. I just want a chance to live a real life...to make something of my life. That's all we all want...a chance to learn to do something and to make something and to be someone...I'd give anything for that."

The evening gave way to night. It was no surprise that after having eaten a little, and before the bottle of wine was finished, they were again making love, and they continued deep into the morning.

THIRTY-TWO

It was early, and Marco was holding Catalina tightly. He strongly desired to protect her and care for her and also felt this deep connection that was indescribable to him. He broke the silence when he could tell she was surfacing from her sleep.

"Catalina, I have to go to work today, but I'd like you to stay here," he said.

"I'd like that," she said. After a long while, she added, "I should probably get some things together, you know. It's hard to find the right thing to wear when you only have one choice!" They laughed together.

"I'll be home early, and perhaps we can have dinner together," he said.

"I don't know, Marco. Maybe we should plan on making love because maybe then we'll actually eat!" At this they both laughed deeply and enjoyed the warmth of their bodies and the splendor of having time together.

Marco rolled out of bed and into the shower first. Before long, he was in a suit and looking spectacular. She admired him from the bed and did little other than watch him move around the flat and get his things together.

"I'll see you tonight," he said as he was walking to the door. She quietly called out to him in the shuffle of opening the door and grabbing the bag that was standing in for his lost briefcase. "Bye!" he said with a crack in his voice as he walked out, not hearing her.

"Bye!" she said as the door closed. "Marco?" He was gone. "I think I love you, Marco Segrato," she said to herself.

He returned home, and as he unlocked the door, he called out to her. There was no answer. He looked around and didn't see any of her stuff. He thought maybe she was playing a hoax, so he made his way into the bedroom, then his bathroom, and then as he returned to the guest room, he became worried. Had he been played? He was certain not. There was nothing out of sorts, and nothing appeared to be missing. No, he was falling in love with Catalina and she with him, he was certain.

He was becoming worried and thought about his options. She had shared a general idea of where she lived with three other women, and he decided it would be best to head that way. It was too far to get there on foot, so he decided to grab a cab.

The driver made his way through traffic on the streets of Buenos Aires, cutting through and around congested areas. Almost an hour later, they came to the neighborhood and housing project he thought was hers. It was massive, spreading across three different blocks. He thought he needed to cross through the first building to a back building. He paid the driver and began walking through to the back structure. There were city noises everywhere, including sirens. As he made his way around a corner, his heart started racing. There were several police units, and police tape demarcated a crime scene. He walked quickly to the location and found one of the officers. He showed the man his ID, said he was with the city attorney's office, and asked whether he could cross through. The cop wasn't sure whether he should let Marco through or not, but he obliged, and Marco began walking to the building.

"What's happened here?" he asked another cop.

"A whore was killed up on the third floor. Some other woman in the apartment shot the pimp, but he's going to live. That's all I know."

Marco was desperate now. He ran into the lobby and was stopped by another officer. "Can I help you?"

"Yes, I am with the city attorney's office." He showed his ID and his business card. "My girlfriend was coming here today to pick up some things. Do we know the names of the victims?"

"Beats me," the cop said.

Marco saw a woman across the lobby of the building. She appeared to have been crying and was being questioned by some men, probably detectives. Marco approached and listened from a few feet away, trying to be discreet. He could hear her answers, but not the investigators' questions.

"I can tell you again. She was already here when I got home this afternoon. She was packing things up and said that she was moving out. It seemed abrupt, and in this place, you need to plan your exit carefully. I asked her what was going on, and she said she'd met a friend and was going stay with him...No, she did not tell me his name, but this was about the same time that our boss showed up looking for his cut. I had mine, but she couldn't produce anything. In fact, she'd been skipping the beat for some time, and it was pissing him off...It means she'd not been turning a lot of tricks, or maybe any tricks. Sometimes I think she was just paying him off with what she could come by and had gone off the wagon...No she wasn't doing drugs or drinking. I mean she wasn't hooking up with customers, wasn't turning tricks...I never knew more than her name, Catalina Valdez. In this business you try not to have many friends; people just get hurt..."

Marco's legs buckled under him, and he caught himself by taking a step forward, away from the witness. He was feeling completely undone, imploded and exploded, numb and on fire. There was nothing stable about his emotional state, and he needed to walk out of the building. He wasn't sure whether he could be in trouble or whether he was culpable or what would happen next. As he left the building, he moved off the walkway to the dead grass in front of the project and hurried his pace. He stopped for a minute to throw up. He wiped his mouth with his sleeve and started walking again. He needed to find a safe place to get ahold of himself.

He was shaking. In shock, he walked for a long time. He just kept walking and walking and paid no attention to where he was. As if by providence, he turned a corner, and through his tears, he saw the most familiar place—the church he'd lived in with Father Diaz shortly after his mother's death. Dazed and confused, grief-stricken and emotionally shattered, he stumbled into the church. As he walked in the front door to the empty sanctuary, all composure that had kept him moving forward left him. He fell to his knees and began to sob loudly. It was as if all of the pain he'd ever experienced was in this one moment, on this one evening, bearing down on him. He was completely washed out, undone, and rinsed away. His mind was fixated on one fact: everyone he'd ever loved was dead. Over and over, this thought circled through his mind, and from this idea, he built a belief that in this moment, he'd been cursed. He felt utter pain, sadness, and despondence as he lay on the floor of an old church, sobbing. It was as if hell's fury had brought him home to Argentina to relive all that had broken his heart fifteen years earlier. His connection to Argentina and his longing to return was just a demon's hoax to make him watch beauty and adoration meet death, as if to bring sport and entertainment to Satan.

His thoughts began to drift to God. "How could I have been abandoned? What God would allow a human, a creation, to experience such dread? How could the Bible, the story of creation, and the lessons I learned in this very sanctuary explain any of the agony welling up in my bones? How could God be a God of love if—"

A hand was gently lain on Marco's back. It rubbed his left shoulder blade softly, which was a spot the cops had struck, as if the hand knew that this spot in particular was bruised deeply, as indeed it was. "My son, why do you weep so? What has brought you such grief?" The man was old and had knelt down slowly because his limbs were not able to support his weight as they once had.

"I loved her! I loved her, and she is gone, stolen…It has happened all over again!" He said as tears cascaded to the floor.

There was a long period of silence. Slowly, given the presence of another soul, Marco regained some composure, coming through the numbing fog of overwhelming loss back to reality. He felt as if he were waking up with a stranger by him. It did not cause him concern but instead was a catalyst to awaken him to the moment. Slowly his mind began to recall where he was and how he'd arrived here. The sanctuary was dark. There was light near the altar, and along the sides, candles burned, often lit by parishioners for lost loved ones. Marco turned to see the stranger's face, which was glowing in the dim light of the candles. As he did so, he wiped his eyes, which were blurry from the tears. Slowly, the man came into view, and Marco recognized Father Diaz. At first, the priest did not make the connection in the dim light. It had been a long time since they had seen each other, and then Marco had been wearing a cap and gown for his law school graduation, well groomed and standing tall and confident.

"Father, it is Marco," he said as he turned to hug the old priest. With this embrace, Marco again began to sob. Father Diaz stood still and hugged his surrogate son tightly, not for a moment interested in knowing why he was crying. He only desired to bring comfort, and as they embraced, Father Diaz prayed that the Father would lift the boy's grief. He asked for peace.

Minutes passed before Marco again found composure. As he did, he began to stand up and helped Father Diaz up as well. "He's aged considerably," Marco thought. This time, Marco collected himself completely. He straightened his clothes and pulled himself together, running his hand through his hair and wiping his eyes to clear them.

"Marco, my son. I believe we need to talk. Please walk me back to my quarters. I think you know where they are, no?" the old priest asked.

Marco laughed. "Of course, Father." The moment broke the hold that grief had on Marco. He was now finally coming out of his despair, and while exhausted, for a moment he was actually able to breathe with relief while still harboring a heavy sadness at Catalina's loss.

THIRTY-THREE

Through the evening, Marco and Father Diaz shared dinner and spoke quietly. Marco did his best to tell the priest all about Catalina and their intense love affair. He held no shame for their actions and shared with Father Diaz that he'd never been so infatuated and intensely connected as he had felt in the past forty-eight hours. He shared in great detail all of their conversations and even their last moments. He also shared that he believed he could have helped her and others like her, had he only had a chance. As the night carried on, he came to the last thing he remembered—the question he'd asked her in the park, and how it had inspired him. In that moment, he thought the two of them would be able to make things happen for people like them who'd been born without opportunity.

Father Diaz listened intently. He asked questions and occasionally shared stories. He opened his own private experiences to Marco—he too had been in love, but his calling had kept him in the church, where he was unable to enjoy a woman's beauty. He was happy that Marco had. Father Diaz believed that God's gift of intimacy between a man and his wife was one of His greatest. Through the night, they laughed together and wept together.

Finally, after a long silence, Father Diaz's body language changed. He seemed to evolve from the weak old man who stood before Marco to the young priest Marco had grown up learning from. "Marco, God places before us all things that challenge our very natures. Do you remember our friend C. S. Lewis?"

"Of course, Father."

"He once said that we can never truly know how great love is without also experiencing the abyss of sorrow and grief. He believed that our experiences, good and bad, define our character. He even used an analogy of a master sculptor who begins with a block of marble and hammers away at it until that which its creator has called forth emerges. No man should ever experience grief as you have. I believe Catalina was a very special and beautiful woman. God knows, too, that I loved your mother and cared for her deeply. While you may not know this, her loss was a moment of great personal sorrow for me, too. But I also know that each of us is called by God to do something that glorifies Him and brings justice to our world. I cannot tell you what you are called to do, but I can tell you this: when you seek your calling and deliver yourself fully to it, these experiences with Catalina and your mother, Magdalena, will play a key role in defining your story. I just pray you will be willing to give yourself to God for that which He is calling you."

Marco spent the night at the church that evening. When he woke up the next morning, grief was still present, but it became perfectly clear why so much had happened to him and why life had taken him where it had. He could see meaning in losing his mother at a young age and in encountering and journeying with Jim Swanson. He now saw why he'd been placed into an elite institution for high school and had later been given the opportunity to go to Georgetown, even though he had felt out of place. "My God, how remarkable," he thought. He saw clearly for the first time the impact these experiences had had on him, as if they had been preparing him. The sum total of little and big things together—the summers with the Swansons and his community of friends from scouting and basketball—had all played a role. He saw all of these years, which had at times left him very much alone and confused, as preparation for something that had been revealed in this moment. He knew why he'd been chosen to work on the mayor's campaign and what he wanted to do with the rest of his life. It was as if God Himself had spoken to him at that moment, saying, "Marco, this is your purpose; this is why you are here."

THIRTY-FOUR

At eighty-three, the old man was moving slowly. But Jim found himself in the pastures almost every day. He didn't ride a horse anymore, but he was able to check out his herd at least once a week, usually with his ranch manager.

As he relaxed one evening and sipped a glass of wine—Malbec of course—he watched Fox News's *Global Report*. On the TV, a crowd was waving familiar light-blue-and-white-striped flags with the coat of arms bearing the sun. The people were celebrating their recent presidential elections.

"Today Argentina has elected a new president, Marco Segrato, who promises to continue the reforms he's pushed forward as governor of Buenos Aires, Argentina's most populous city and home to almost half of the country's population. Governor Segrato has brought industry from neighboring countries as well as many United States–based businesses that are looking to tap into South America's vibrant markets. A lifelong civil servant, Marco is also the country's first unmarried president. He's considered to be one of the world's conservative leaders, and he will likely continue to push for reforms that his campaign boasted would strengthen Argentina by strengthening the rule of law, enhancing education, and providing people more opportunities to rise in class and socioeconomic status. US President Kollorse called the president-elect to congratulate him and expressed her interest in continuing to enhance the partnership between the two countries by strengthening ties and investing in the region's economic future," a reporter said.

Jim smiled as he pondered this. He thought about the years leading to his success and how a single encounter had changed everything for him. His client Jose Carlo Segrato wanted to raise descendants who would one day lead his country; he gave a peasant boy a name. Jim Swanson was lost and wanted to find purpose in his life; he rescued an orphan. Marco Segrato wanted to help his mother find her way out of the slums; he led a nation to work and gave the poor a chance to live better lives. "Three men and their legacies," thought Jim Swanson.

EPILOGUE

I have my black tie on; I'm sitting at the head table with the president of the United States and her husband.

"Madam President, do you mind if I call my attaché over briefly?" I ask.

"Certainly!" she says.

I raise my hand slightly; there are eyes everywhere. Between the secret service personnel and my own security detail, every movement is best played out slowly, for fear I might make someone nervous. A moment later, my assistant is by my side.

"I want to detour when we leave. I'd like to see whether we can make an unannounced stop in Arkansas, or at least not publically disclose it. What do we need to do?"

She is confused and looks at me like I am crazy. "Sir?"

I am reminded again of Elizabeth Taylor. "We are sitting next to the President of the United States. If there are some obstacles, we can more than likely get through them if we ask right now. Just see what they say and report back to me."

I can tell President Kollorse is trying to be discreet as she leans over. "Is everything all right?" she asks.

"Lois, I need to ask a favor, please. It might ruffle a few feathers, send up a few flares, freak out the secret service, and send the

Arkansas National Guard into red alert, but it would mean a lot to me."

"What?" she asks smiling, almost laughing.

"I want to see a dear friend. Well, he's almost like a father to me. Can we arrange for me to blow in and out of Arkansas and make a stop at his ranch?"

Kollorse knows the story. "Jim Swanson? You bet, Mr. President. That we can definitely make happen." She waves to her own staff. "Get the chief of staff over here pronto, Andrew."

"Yes, ma'am!" The young lieutenant in full regalia dashes off to set things in motion.